Izar shouldn't have engaged with her. He shouldn't have listened to a word she said, because how could it matter? And who cared if the woman who was still his duty had gone and transformed herself into the physical manifestation of his deepest desires?

That he noticed at all was appalling. He'd have to add that to his laundry list of reasons to loathe himself. Later.

But in that moment, Izar did more than notice. He let his eyes drift down to Liliana's lips and linger there. Almost as if he was powerless to help himself—or stop.

"Oh," she said softly, and the word was ripe with too many meanings. Revelation and understanding. Something like wonder. A touch of daring besides, and it poured through him, molten hot and impossible to resist. "Honey, not vinegar. I should have realized. The great and terrible Izar Agustin only *acts* tough."

She threw herself forward and into him, catching herself with her palms flat against his chest even as his hands came up to grip her upper arms. Automatically, he told himself. To push her away, he told himself—but he didn't.

Her skin was every bit as smooth to the touch as he'd tried not to imagine. The contact was like fire, surging through him, making him insane enough to understand he was hot and hard and unwilling to do a damn thing to change it—

And then Liliana surged up onto her toes and pressed her lips to his.

## One Night With Consequences

*When one night...leads to pregnancy!*

When succumbing to a night of unbridled desire,
it's impossible to think past the morning after!

But with the sheets barely settled, that little blue line
appears on the pregnancy test, and it doesn't take
long to realize that one night of white-hot passion has
turned into a lifetime of consequences!

Only one question remains:

How do you tell a man you've just met that you're
about to share more than just his bed?

Find out in:

*An Illicit Night with the Greek* by Susanna Carr

*A Vow to Secure His Legacy* by Annie West

*Bound to the Tuscan Billionaire* by Susan Stephens

*The Shock Cassano Baby* by Andie Brock

*The Greek's Nine-Month Redemption* by Maisey Yates

*An Heir to Make A Marriage* by Abby Green

*Crowned for the Prince's Heir* by Sharon Kendrick

*The Sheikh's Baby Scandal* by Carol Marinelli

*A Ring for Vincenzo's Heir* by Jennie Lucas

*Claiming His Christmas Consequence* by Michelle Smart

Look for more **One Night With Consequences**
coming soon!

# *Caitlin Crews*

———

# THE GUARDIAN'S
# VIRGIN WARD

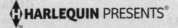

HARLEQUIN PRESENTS®

Recycling programs
for this product may
not exist in your area.

ISBN-13: 978-0-373-13969-9

The Guardian's Virgin Ward

First North American Publication 2016

Copyright © 2016 by Caitlin Crews

This is a work of fiction. Names, characters, places and incidents are either the product of the author's imagination or are used fictitiously, and any resemblance to actual persons, living or dead, business establishments, events or locales is entirely coincidental.

This edition published by arrangement with Harlequin Books S.A.

For questions and comments about the quality of this book, please contact us at CustomerService@Harlequin.com.

Printed in U.S.A.

*USA TODAY* bestselling and RITA® Award–nominated author **Caitlin Crews** loves writing romance. She teaches her favourite romance novels in creative writing classes at places like UCLA Extension's prestigious Writers' Program, where she finally gets to utilize the MA and PhD in English literature she received from the University of York in England. She currently lives in California, with her very own hero and too many pets. Visit her at caitlincrews.com.

### Books by Caitlin Crews

### Harlequin Presents

*Castelli's Virgin Widow*
*At the Count's Bidding*
*Undone by the Sultan's Touch*
*Not Just the Boss's Plaything*
*A Devil in Disguise*

### The Billionaire's Legacy

*The Return of the Di Sione Wife*

### Wedlocked!

*Expecting a Royal Scandal*

### The Chatsfield

*Greek's Last Redemption*

### Scandalous Sheikh Brides

*Protecting the Desert Heir*
*Traded to the Desert Sheikh*

### Vows of Convenience

*His for a Price*
*His for Revenge*

### Royal and Ruthless

*A Royal Without Rules*

Visit the Author Profile page at Harlequin.com for more titles.

USA TODAY bestselling and RITA® Award–nominated author Caitlin Crews loves writing romance. She teaches her favourite romance novels in creative writing classes at places like UCLA Extension's prestigious Writers' Program, where she finally gets to utilise the MA and PhD in English literature she received from the University of York in England. She currently lives in California, with her comedian husband and their menagerie of ridiculous animals.

### Books by Caitlin Crews

#### Harlequin Presents

Pregnant by the Desert King

The Bride's Baby of Shame
At the Count's Bidding

The Billionaire's Secret Princess
Shameless

*Scandalous Royal Brides*
The Prince's Nine-Month Scandal
Expecting a Royal Scandal

*Vows of Convenience*
His for a Price
His for Revenge

*Royal and Ruthless*
A Royal Without Rules
A Scandal in the Headlines
A Devil in Disguise

Visit the Author Profile page at millsandboon.com.au for more titles.

# CHAPTER ONE

"THIS PARTY IS finally looking like the birthday gift to you it's supposed to be, Lily!"

Liliana's roommate Kay was practically shivering with glee as she bounded into the narrow kitchen, which was normal for her even in the middle of the loud, crowded party they were currently hosting in their Bronx, New York apartment.

"The most beautiful man I've ever seen in my entire life just walked into our living room and asked for you. You promised you were going to change your life, remember?" Kay grinned and let her smile go a little bit salacious. "And believe me when I tell you that doing anything at all with this particular man will not be a hardship."

Liliana Girard Brooks, who'd gone by Lily Bertrand since she'd started college, to put a little space between her brand-new life and her internationally recognizable name with all that history attached to it, had vowed earlier that chilly November evening that her twenty-third birthday party was going to change her boring, stiflingly barren existence as a latter-day nun once and for all.

She hadn't really expected to have an opportunity to keep that vow. Especially this early in the night.

"You're finally going to lose your virginity!" her second roommate Jules had cried over pizza, punching her fist in the air as punctuation. This was also normal. "Welcome to the twenty-first century at last!"

"You don't have to lose anything," Kay countered, frowning at Jules when Liliana had frozen solid where she sat with a slice of pepperoni halfway to her mouth. "You don't have to do anything you don't want to do."

"The other side of that being you can do anything you *do* want to do, once and for all," Jules had retorted, wholly unchastened.

"Don't worry," Liliana had replied, opting not to remind her roommates that she'd only ever been kissed once during their senior year in college, and it had been embarrassing for everyone concerned. They knew that. Sometimes it felt as if the entire population of New York City knew that, too. "My ugly-duckling years are over. I hereby declare that tonight is the night I'll transform into a swan at last!"

They'd all cheered and hugged, then turned up the music, and Liliana had channeled her shaky certainty into her wineglass, where she'd helped herself to far more white wine than was usual for a girl who had believed it when the terrifying headmistress at her prison-like boarding school in Switzerland had told her wine made women into whores.

"Is that the legacy you wish to build as the last living heir to two mighty bloodlines?" Madame had asked with stern distaste, as if Liliana had already been discovered turning tricks on the shores of Lake Geneva. At that time Liliana had been fourteen and far more concerned with the solo careers of certain former boy band members than *mighty bloodlines* of any description. Particularly her own. "There are any number of rich, vacuous whores cluttering up the tabloids. It is up to you whether you wish to make a spectacle of yourself in this way or not."

Here in the safety of their tiny kitchen, Liliana toasted her former prison warden and her roommate's expectant expression with one lift of her glass, then took a deep pull from it.

*Sweet white wine,* she thought happily. Maybe too happily. *Making ugly ducklings into swans since the first grape was crushed underfoot.*

If only in her own head.

"This is the new and improved Lily Bertrand

you're looking at," she told Kay grandly and with a great deal of confidence she didn't actually feel. "Beautiful men are nothing but my due."

"Damn right," Kay replied. She nudged Liliana with her shoulder. "But you might have to leave the kitchen to collect what's owed you, you know."

Liliana did not want to leave the kitchen. The party was loud and silly and as vaguely unsettling as all parties always seemed to her. It was also packed full of the approximately seventeen million friends Kay and Jules had made during their years at Barnard.

Liliana, by contrast, had made exactly two friends at Barnard: Kay and Jules.

*Wine,* she reminded herself as she forced herself out of the narrow galley kitchen and edged her way into the crowded living room. *Wine understands. Wine is here to help.*

She took another sip. Okay, maybe it was a gulp. Either way, it made leaving the relative safety of the kitchen feel a whole lot more like a powerful choice she was opting to make instead of a terrifying dare she had no choice but to perform, thanks to her big mouth.

Luckily, the more she drank, the more mellow she felt and the less she cared about the consequences of ill-considered vow-making. Almost as if everything she'd said—and, yes, foolishly vowed—to her roommates tonight was true, instead of little more than wishful thinking. And maybe alcohol didn't disagree with her after all, the way Liliana had always claimed it did because that minor lie was easier than admitting that a dour Frenchwoman she hadn't seen since her high school graduation still took up so much real estate in her head.

*It's not just Madame who's cluttering things up in here*, a small voice reminded her then, but she shoved that aside. The last thing she wanted to think about was the impossible, overwhelming guardian who made his presence felt from afar with such ease. Not here. Certainly not now.

The edges of the funky apartment, tucked away in a more creative than strictly safe part of the Bronx, began to blur in a pleasant sort of way. Liliana dared to imagine herself a little bit blurrily, as well, as the carefree and intrepid girl she'd always daydreamed she might have been had she not been locked away in the strictest finishing school in Europe throughout her lonely childhood. The kind of girl who was as easygoing as her roommates, perfectly capable of charging up to a man deemed beautiful by her friends to announce that it was his lucky night, because he'd been declared her birthday present.

Maybe it wasn't that she was a freak and a

weirdo for never really indulging in the kinds of romantic adventures her friends had repeatedly had throughout their college years and were still having this first year after graduation. Maybe it wasn't that she was gangly and awkward at best when infamous heiresses were meant to be as effortlessly chic and beautiful as her own mother had been, forever standing in as revered muses for fashion designers or draping themselves on the arms of movie stars. Tonight, inching into her own living room despite the fact it was packed with strangers, and letting the wine do its good work this once, Liliana toyed with the notion that maybe—just maybe—she'd simply never given herself the *opportunity* to explore the less prim and buttoned-up side of herself that she was positive was lurking inside of her somewhere.

It had taken at least two years out of boarding school to stop imagining that Madame would appear the way she always had in the Chateau to strike Liliana down for any and all inappropriate or not entirely ladylike thoughts.

"Your mouth belongs in the gutters," Madame had always told the girls who'd defied her. "Perhaps it is you who belong there, too."

It had taken another couple of years for Liliana to relax enough to dare to *say* the things that she thought, if only to her very few, carefully chosen friends. And it was only now, at the beginning of her sixth month after graduating from Barnard, that Liliana felt as if she finally had the faintest notion of who she really was once she let herself relax into her life.

For one thing, she was no longer the sad, locked-away-in-a-tower heiress. No longer marked by the great Girard and Brooks fortunes she would one day control. She might always be famous for the sudden, shocking loss of her parents and her subsequent banishment to a European boarding school at the direction of the famously ruthless and remote guardian she hardly knew, just as she would always be known for the vast wealth her blue-blooded mother and corporate-giant father had left her.

But Liliana had put a lot of distance between her real life and those pathetic stories of the poor little rich girl she'd been considered all her life, trotted out in every exasperating article or television program and compared to this or that member of the Onassis family. Or sometimes even Rapunzel. She'd deliberately used one of her mother's little-known family names as her surname these past four-and-a-half years, and she lived well below the radar in the Bronx with her friends, indistinguishable from every other young woman in the throes of her very first job after college.

She wasn't on a reality show set in the Hollywood wastelands or taking up space on various yachts in Cannes. She was definitely not one of the tabloid heiresses Madame had predicted she'd become if left to her own devices. When magazines inevitably listed her on this or that collection of billionaire heiresses, they almost always referred to her as *low-key* and sometimes even *reclusive*, which was exactly what she wanted. The best she could hope for, even.

And if Liliana suspected that really, she was desperate to prove that she wasn't the useless creature her legal guardian—the eternally disapproving Izar Agustin, beloved by most of Europe and revered like a freshly minted saint in his native Spain, where he also happened to be one of its wealthiest citizens—always intimated she was in the curt and sometimes outright rude letters and emails that served as his preferred form of very distant communication with her over these ten years, well. It didn't matter *why*, surely. It only mattered that she was neither cluttering up the tabloids nor making herself a burden on the dark, harsh guardian who still controlled the bulk of her fortune.

From afar, which was likely a blessing, since she hadn't laid eyes on the man since the terrible day he'd introduced himself as her new legal guardian and had then shipped her off to boarding school. Not in person, anyway.

It turned out that not even wine could protect her from thoughts of Izar. They crept in like the heat from the cranky old radiators in this prewar apartment, almost sullen at first, than with force and authority. A great deal like Izar himself, she imagined, though Liliana doubted *he* crept anywhere he could stride powerfully, instead.

In her head, he was mighty and overwhelming, like a titan. A god. All-powerful and all-knowing.

Visions of Izar's trademark black gaze and that cutting, mocking curl of his haughty lips—always splashed across all the tabloids—flashed through her and made something deep inside her flip over, then hum. For years this man she never saw had dominated Liliana's thoughts and dreams alike, either as she'd fumed over his latest stark, pointed communication or waited months and months for the next.

"No yachts in the Mediterranean. You are not a call girl, to my knowledge," he'd written when she'd dutifully requested his permission to spend the summer with a few boarding-school friends, exploring the French Riviera and possibly heading on to the Greek isles.

She'd been seventeen. And she'd spent that

summer the way she'd spent most of her holidays and breaks, in the halls of the Chateau working on an independent study project with the rest of the forgotten and unwanted students. The upside was she'd had an extraordinary amount of extra credit to dangle before colleges when she'd applied.

For a man she hadn't seen since the worst day of her life, who'd abandoned her into the care of Madame and the rest of the severe teachers at school, Izar still managed to exert an iron control over her life.

Liliana shuddered, pressing her back to the exposed brick wall that took up one side of her small living room as she gazed out at all the merry, happy people her roommates had invited tonight. If there was a beautiful man who would change her life—or at least make it more interesting—in the tight scrum of them, she couldn't see him. All she could see was Izar.

The story of her life. And she was sick of it.

No matter how many fawning pseudojournalists wrote him love letters disguised as breathless, flattering profiles in major magazines—and there were always at least three per season, it seemed—Izar remained famously unattainable. A legend. Driven and focused, above all things. Women were candy to him; easily consumed and even more easily forgotten. Some of the corporations he bought and sold were the same.

Of all the independent study projects Liliana had undertaken, her research into Izar Agustin was the one to which she'd devoted the most attention over the years. She knew all of his biographical details by heart and not one of them made his controlling yet hands-off treatment of her any easier to bear.

A Spanish *fútbol* player in his late teens and early twenties, Izar had dominated the pitch before he'd blown out his knee in the final moments of a dramatic championship match—which that career-ending kick had won, of course. Instead of descending into despair and obscurity, Izar had made what many had considered a strange sort of pivot at the time and had charged into the luxury goods business, instead, joining forces with Liliana's parents a few years later. Together, they'd controlled the prestigious fashion house that had been in her French mother's family for generations, the international Brooks wine and tobacco interests that Liliana's South African grandfather had transitioned into a luxury goods conglomerate, and Izar's own collection of sports and active lifestyle concerns. Agustin Brooks Girard had rapidly become a force to be reckoned with, and then Liliana's parents had died in that accident, leaving Izar in charge of everything—including Liliana herself, their only child and heir.

Izar had been her guardian in all ways until she turned twenty-one, a role he'd executed as a dark shadow over her life rather than any kind of part of it. These days he merely controlled the company, in which her parents had left her their equal interest, until she turned twenty-five or was married.

Liliana comforted herself with the knowledge that once she controlled the whole of her own fortune and the shares and responsibilities that came with it, she'd have the opportunity to treat Izar the way he'd always treated her. As if he was little more than an unpleasant thing she'd stepped on en route to something far more worthy of her time and attention. She had involved fantasies of sending him snide notes every seven months or so, the better to demonstrate her patronizing disinterest.

*I would rather drink cyanide than support your proposal*, she fantasized about writing him one day. *But thank you*.

Childish, maybe. But that was the point. She'd actually been a child ten years ago. Would it have killed the famously intense and ruthless Izar to be a bit kinder to his late business partners' daughter that awful day? Liliana been suddenly, cruelly left all alone in the world when her parents' private plane had gone down some-where over the Pacific. She'd been twelve years old, made of equal parts puppy fat and terrible pain, and nothing bad had ever happened to her before. She might have been sheltered—but weren't twelve-year-old girls *supposed* to be a little bit sheltered, if at all possible? She under-stood that Izar might have been a bit young for sudden-onset parenting, being just under thirty himself and used to a rather more exciting life-style than one including an orphaned preteen, presumably, but had it *really* been necessary to remove her from the only home she'd known in England to install her in that harsh and hateful school in Switzerland? And then leave her there to rot without a single visit ever after?

"Hate me if you feel you must," Izar had told her in his cold, measured, immovable way, his native Spanish making the words seem warmer than they were. Right there in the foyer of the house she'd spent her entire life in mere mo-ments after he'd ordered the staff to pack up all her things. Twelve-year-old Liliana had been certain she was looking at the devil himself, all hellfire black eyes, that Roman coin of a nose, and the brooding way he'd stared down at her. A muscle in his lean cheek had clenched once. Then again. "I am your guardian whether you like it or do not, and your feelings cannot affect my decisions. You will do as I say, regardless."

And she had, of course. What choice had there been?

"Get a hold of yourself," Liliana muttered to herself now. She only realized she'd spoken out loud when she heard her own voice against the indie darling band currently crooning from the speakers, and she flushed. Then hoped that the music had drowned her out—because her roommates' friends already thought she was a bit off, she was aware. They didn't need any further evidence.

Izar had not been impressed with her decision to attend college in the States instead of the horrifying wannabe convent he'd had in mind in the far reaches of the European Alps. He'd grudgingly allowed it when she'd promised him that she was only applying to what few all-women colleges remained in America. Then he had very nearly rescinded his permission entirely, because he certainly hadn't been pleased at the idea that she'd be living in New York City, known den of iniquity, once she'd made her final choice.

He'd even called, the rare gesture underscoring the depths of his misgivings. Or more accurately, one of his aides had called, then demanded she hold until he could sweep onto the line like a tornado.

"If there is so much as a whisper of scandal connected to you, Liliana, you will regret it," he'd told her in a quietly menacing tone that had made every hair on her body stand on end. "I will pull you out of that college myself, with my own two hands, and you will not enjoy the consequences. Do you understand me?"

"You rarely leave much room for misunderstanding," she'd replied, wisely making her voice meek rather than foolishly defiant at the last moment. That she'd dared even that much had made her stomach flip over. "Sir."

There had been nothing but silence for far too long and she'd been sure that she'd gone too far. That he would consign her to another prison term in another school so far away from the world she'd never learn how to live in it. That there was no escape from the brooding shadow he cast over her life.

"I'll allow it," he'd said eventually, so grudging and dark Liliana was amazed the phone receiver in her hand didn't freeze. "On a provisional basis only."

She'd marked it as a victory, and who cared if it was a narrow one.

But he was the one winning in the end, she realized now, as she was still standing there like a fool with her back against her own living room wall. Izar had two years left to interfere in her life as he pleased, but he wasn't here in her apartment tonight. The very idea was laughable. First, she hadn't exactly been forthcoming about where she was living these days. And second, Izar had never visited her. Ever. He hadn't made contact in months.

She told herself that hollow sensation, deep inside, was relief.

*Why on earth do you want his recognition?* a little voice asked from somewhere inside that hollowness. *You shouldn't. You should want him to go away and leave you alone, forever.*

She told herself she did, and no matter that such a thing would never happen. Of course she did.

Because she couldn't possibly want the attention of the man who'd abandoned her as a child. Certainly not. That would be clichéd and silly and deeply, unutterably sad, and Liliana was finished being any of those things.

At that, she launched herself into the crowd, scanning the room for anyone Kay might consider the most beautiful man she'd ever seen in her life. There were any number of contenders, this being New York City and basically ground zero for Kay's sort of dream man—but no. Jules was over near the bookcase in her usual throng of admirers, and she jerked her head in a wholly unsubtle manner toward the small bit of the L-shaped living room when Liliana caught her eye. That was the part of the common area that led into their three railroad-style bedrooms, stacked one on top of the next so only the farthest back had any real privacy. They'd drawn straws for the back bedroom when they'd moved in and Liliana had won it, which she'd had a lot of time to regret in these past months. The privacy was nice, sure, but it meant that she spent a lot of time creeping through Jules's and Kay's bedrooms, pretending with all her might not to see what might or might not be happening in their beds after their giddy nights out.

She waved an acknowledgment at Jules and obediently made her way through the clumps of merrymaking people until she pushed through the first bedroom door. It was quieter in Jules's room, though only slightly. A large, spirited group of people—including a few women Liliana recognized from Barnard—were piled on the bed, laughing as they watched something on a laptop.

"Keep going," one of the Barnard women said when she saw Liliana, flashing a knowing sort of grin. "Jules told him to wait for you in private."

Liliana was beginning to wonder if her roommates had done something unforgivably humiliating, like hire one of those male strippers Jules was always threatening to unleash upon her. Liliana flushed at the very idea. She'd barely survived that sloppy, awful kiss her senior year. A naked, dancing man was likely to send her to the hospital.

*You really are pathetic, aren't you?* a hard voice that greatly resembled her memory of her guardian's asked from deep inside her.

She hated that voice.

Liliana wrenched open Kay's door—but there was no one there. Not a soul on the queen-sized futon that took up almost all the available floor space in the tiny room, so she pulled in a breath that was shakier than she wanted to admit and tiptoed around it toward the door to her own bedroom.

A sense of foreboding swept through her when she put her hand on her own doorknob, a prickling sort of chill that washed over her from her scalp to her heels, then back. Surely her friends wouldn't embarrass her. They never had in all the time she'd known and lived with them, here or in their suite at college. And Lord knew she'd always been the easiest of targets. She thought back, but she hadn't seen the faintest shred of that particular, pointed glee in either of her friends' expressions that might suggest a practical joke was in the offing.

Still, she stood rooted to the spot outside her own bedroom, that odd hum deep in her belly shivering through her, as if her body knew things she didn't.

Liliana didn't like that feeling at all.

But she kept going because she'd promised she would. And because she was tired of being the odd one out. The ugly, awkward duckling. The strange creature her friends were forever apologizing for when she would do yet another thing that marked her as *different*. Unworldly. Naive. Set apart, always.

Liliana wasn't convinced she'd ever transform into a swan in any real sense. She was the daughter of one of the most beautiful and fashionable women who had ever lived, so she knew what a swan looked like and how far from the mark she was in comparison. Try miles upon miles, and then some. But that was okay. She'd settle for becoming a sparrow. Something with wings and no fear of heights, so she could finally put her family history and her tragic past behind her.

That was the thought that had her throwing open her door and stepping into her own bedroom at last.

Her room was exactly as she'd left it, save

the tall figure that stood still and dark at her windows, looking out toward the chaotic street below. With his clothes on, thankfully, and no sign of a telltale boom box like all the movies. Her heart tripped over itself and she glanced around quickly to make sure there was nothing in her private space that would make her seem as much of a weirdo as she knew she was, as everyone always told her she was. Everything seemed in order. Her neatly made bed was on one wall and her desk on the other, with nothing but her laptop and the latest novel she was reading on the surface and more books stacked neatly on the shelves above it. She'd left her closet door half-open earlier, but there was nothing inside but her meticulously hung and carefully folded clothes. No mess, inside the closet or the bedroom itself. No pictures. No art. Just the brick wall on one side and the weathered windows on the other.

It had never occurred to Liliana before that instant that it might as well be one of the dorm rooms she'd lived in over the years. Or a nun's little cell in a convent, for that matter. *Or a prison*, a small voice interjected inside of her. It was that stark and without particular character, unlike her roommates' rooms, which *exploded* with their dispositions and possessions spilling across every available surface, from their bright comforters to their trinkets and clothes to the posters that decorated their walls.

But she didn't have time to process that, much less think about what it said about her. Because the man who stood with his back to her, staring out at the Bronx and the mad glitter of Manhattan off in the distance through the half-fogged windows, turned.

And nothing made sense.

Her heart stopped. Then began again, with a kick that made the room spin around and then center somewhere deep in her belly, where she felt raw and hollow at once.

Because it was Izar.

The cruel and terrible Izar that Liliana had only seen in photographs for years. The guardian she'd always found equal parts maddening and horrible no matter how little she heard from him. She'd spent hours upon hours studying the man from afar, looking for proof that he was as terrible as she thought he was. And in all that time she'd never thought of him as anything but the remote and inaccessible bane of her existence. The shadow hanging over her, that was it.

But Kay had called him beautiful.

Izar could not be beautiful. Izar was… Izar. Nothing more.

But the damage was already done.

Suddenly, Liliana found herself completely unable to see the same dark, fairy-tale monster she'd always imagined when she'd thought of this man. She'd told herself she hated him and had imagined herself the wronged innocent in a tale that could only end with the big, bad wolf finally getting his comeuppance. She'd imagined him *getting his* in a great variety of ways, in fact. And it wasn't that the real, live Izar was any less a devil than she'd imagined as he stood there, making no attempt to hide his disapproval from her as he frowned at her.

But suddenly—impossibly, irrevocably—all she could see was the fact he was also a man.

Because whatever else Izar was, whatever she'd told herself all this time because she'd needed to believe it as she'd scowled at all those pictures of him, he was indisputably a man.

Something red and furious swept through Liliana then, making her much too hot and suddenly desperately worried that her skin might crack wide open with the force of it. Her head felt light. Her knees seemed weak. And deep in her core, she melted.

Izar was formed like the bronze statue of himself that she knew very well stood in the impoverished Spanish neighborhood where he'd grown up. He was all hard male sinew and restless, brooding grace that shouted out his ingrained athleticism without him having to say a single word or move a muscle. He was dressed in the sort of sleek, impossibly chic and yet relentlessly masculine way he favored, broadcasting the fact he ran an empire that included some of the world's best-loved couture houses while failing, somehow, to mute that elemental power of his that came off of him in waves.

Most of that was obvious in the pictures she'd seen of him.

In person, he was like a blast of winter wind. Intense. Ruthless. Undeniable.

He was muscled and perfect, and then there was that fallen angel's face of his—all dark brows and his close-cropped dark hair, the scrape of the day's beard on his belligerent jaw, and those acrobatic cheekbones that made his arrogant mouth, hard and yet full, nothing short of breathtaking.

Literally, it stole her breath.

*He did.*

That hum deep inside of her started again, making her skin prickle all over and a giddy sort of shiver wind through her belly, tight and sharp.

Izar didn't make sense in her bedroom. He'd been bad enough in her head. He was lean for such a big, strong man, reminding her of the clips she'd seen of him on the *fútbol* pitch, all that hungry and focused grace mixed with impossible speed—

What was happening to her?

His dark gaze fastened on hers and seemed to burn through her. Her cheeks flushed redder and her stomach kept up its maddening shiver and hum, and she was suddenly panicked at the thought of what might happen. What he might do if he ever suspected what was happening to her. What she felt—careening around inside of her, bright and impossible—

"You are no longer twelve," he bit out, and his voice in person was…better. Richer. Darker. Delicious, somehow.

God help her. She was definitely no longer twelve.

And she refused to act as if she still was, no matter that the fairy-tale shadows in her head had come to life before her eyes…and in a way that was far more raw and real than she ever could have imagined.

"My friends said my birthday present was waiting for me in here," Liliana said, with an ease that had to be all about the wine she'd been drinking, because it certainly wasn't her usual way of speaking. To anyone, and especially not to him—not that she'd had much practice with the latter. "If they meant you, it's official. This is the worst birthday of my life."

Izar took a step toward her, then stopped abruptly. As if he didn't quite trust himself to come closer—but that was ridiculous. Still, the odd little notion made her throat go dry and her heart beat at her all the harder.

His black eyes glittered in the buttery light from her desk lamp and the chaotic gleam of the city outside her windows. He held himself still, so still she was entirely too aware of his solid shoulders, which took up the whole of her bedroom, and how he seemed to vibrate with a certain rich, masculine darkness that kicked its way along her limbs and pooled deep in her belly. Then pulsed.

But this wasn't a letter. This wasn't one of the few, brief telephone calls they'd had over the years in which he spoke and she was expected to listen gratefully and then quietly obey. This was her bedroom and her birthday party.

This was her life.

And she didn't have to be cowed by this man, no matter the effect he had on her and no matter what parts of her fortune and future he still controlled.

"Did you by any chance happen upon a better-looking man and heave him out the windows? Into the closet?" She smiled at Izar. Coolly. Which was not the snide note of her dreams but felt good all the same. "Because I left my own birthday party for the promise of a hot guy, not you." She let her smile deepen, trying to look as unimpressed with him as possible. *"Sir."*

A muscle in Izar's lean jaw clenched. And she was not at all prepared for his thunderous scowl. It all seemed directly wired to that pulsing, humming, molten place between her legs.

"Tell me something, Liliana," her guardian said very distinctly. Fury and something far darker and more dangerous threaded through that quiet voice of his she'd only heard directed at her once or twice in all these years. And never like this, as if he had feelings about her one way or the other. She could hardly breathe through it. "What game do you imagine you are playing?"

# CHAPTER TWO

THE LAST TIME Izar Agustin had seen Liliana Girard Brooks in the flesh, she'd been young and flushed and sobbing her eyes out. Not unreasonable for a girl who had lost her parents, but entirely outside his various areas of expertise. Then, as now, he'd acted entirely in her best interests—none of which could possibly have included welcoming her into his high-profile, business-focused, notably tearless life.

Liliana was the heiress to an unimaginable fortune and half of his company. She was his ward and his responsibility. In his head she had remained that chubby, awkward and soddenfaced child he'd met all those years ago, no matter that he'd been well aware she'd grown older in the interim. And tonight she was standing there before him entirely grown-up and dressed like a common whore.

And, moreover, had just talked back to him in a manner reminiscent of the streetwalking variety of the same, if his ears had not deceived him and his memories of the unsavory neighborhoods of his youth did not fail him.

Izar couldn't quite take it all in. He couldn't *quite* fathom it, because this level of crude defiance spoke to a failure on his part so deep it should have leveled him. And it was a simple fact that Izar was too unaccustomed to the experience of failure to tell one way or the other.

Her attire was not the worst part. Nor was the fact that she was here at all, apparently *living* in this ramshackle, flea-bitten flat four rickety flights up in a building she could have purchased outright with the change in her pocket—though that factored. It was that she'd deliberately lied to him about where she was living in this sinful city, making Izar's trek into the hinterland of questionable neighborhoods in the Bronx, of all places, unavoidable on a night he'd intended to spend in more civilized pursuits, such as the theater with one of his current mistresses.

Izar Agustin—who prided himself on his iron control and ruthless focus in all things, from the *fútbol* pitch of his youth to his current domination of any boardroom he entered—had allowed this situation to get out of control. Clearly. Yes, Liliana had lied to him. Yes, she had gone to some lengths to deliberately mislead him, allowing him to believe that she'd spent these months since her college graduation living in her late parents' brownstone in the deeply moneyed and far less dangerous West Village in Manhattan rather than here in this grotty hinterland. Still, he could blame no one but himself.

Not even the woman who stood before him, sulky-mouthed and flushed from what appeared to be equal parts defiance and drink, glaring at him as if he was the devil incarnate.

Izar supposed he was. As far as Liliana was concerned, he was far worse. And he was about to rain down a little brimstone all over her to cement that impression.

"Do you have anything to say for yourself?" He kept his voice soft. Low. He did nothing to conceal the harsh lash of it that regularly made his underlings and associates cower, stammer and fall all over themselves to apologize no matter if they were guilty of anything or not.

His ward only tipped up her chin as if he'd landed a glancing blow at best. And as if she expected—even welcomed—more. He couldn't remember the last time he'd seen anything like it. This was not how people treated a man of his stature. Ever.

"Nothing polite," she retorted.

It took Izar one beat, then another, to understand that it was temper that wound through him, red and wild, at her bored and disinterested tone. *Temper*, when he hadn't permitted himself anything close to such a display of emotion since he'd left *fútbol* behind him.

It was there in his tone when he spoke. "You cannot possibly imagine that adding insults, however vague, to your deceit and your dishonesty—to say nothing of your appalling disregard for your own safety—is the correct way to handle this situation, can you?"

He could hear the fury in his voice slice through the room, but Liliana didn't flinch. She didn't crumble or break. Izar had taken down whole companies with a far gentler tone than the one he'd used on her, but Liliana didn't appear to notice it.

Izar couldn't decide if he admired her or wanted to throttle her for that. He only knew that neither feeling was the least bit appropriate.

"The only situation I'm aware of is that there's an uninvited guest lurking in my bedroom," she replied, with a level of icy hauteur that would have done a queen proud.

It almost diverted his attention from the fact she'd accused him of *lurking*. He was Izar Agustin. He did not *lurk*.

Nor was she finished. "I'd like you to leave. Now."

Liliana wasn't a child any longer. The grown-up version stood before him with the carriage of the aristocrat she was, though one would hardly know it surrounded by the relentless, depressing squalor of this place. He'd grown up in a shoddy flat a great deal like this one, if across the world in the outskirts of Málaga, Spain, and he'd vowed he'd never sully himself in such places again. That he'd had no choice in the matter tonight only made his temper that much more precarious. Liliana was entirely too soft and vulnerable to be prancing about in a down-market flat in a questionable section of the Bronx, regardless of her net worth. But the fact that she was *Liliana Girard Brooks* meant that every time she exposed herself on the unpleasant streets in this neighborhood she made herself a juicy target for any enterprising fortune hunter or kidnapper or miscreant of any description who happened along.

It made him well nigh murderous.

But the questionable neighborhood wasn't the only problem.

Maturity had brought out those pedigreed cheekbones of hers, which in turn made the seemingly haphazard way she'd styled her masses of golden hair on the top of her head look that much more elegant and chic. The kind of effortless style women the world over spent lifetimes trying and failing to attain. She'd shed her youthful roundness altogether and had finally grown into the interesting face that had been far too much for her at twelve, with all those edges and angles the camera would worship. Taller, slimmer, and far more at ease in her own body than he remembered her, Liliana was nothing short of mesmerizing. All her finely etched angles worked with the sophisticated sweep of dark lashes framing her faintly tilted blue eyes and the sleek curves of her lean body, hitting him like a sucker punch. Hard. And then there was that plump, sweet mouth of hers that, God help him, he felt like a carnal wallop in his gut. And lower still.

This could not be happening.

He never thought of Liliana as anything but his responsibility. His task to complete, nothing more. Her parents would have wanted her to have the business and fortune they'd left her, and so Izar had honored them by making sure both not only existed but thrived. Her looks hadn't signified. She'd been a child in his mind all this time, entrusted to his care and in need of his firm, if distant, guidance.

But she wasn't a child now.

Liliana was truly and indisputably beautiful, little as he wished to acknowledge such a thing. She was more than simply beautiful, if he was being honest with himself. Without his permission and entirely against his wishes, Liliana had blossomed into one of the most stunning women he'd ever seen in his life. He thought she surpassed even her own mother, the lost and much-lamented style icon Clothilde Girard, who was still held to be one of the great, elegant beauties of her time a decade after her death.

Maybe it was the fact Liliana was flouting his authority by her presence here at all. It was the first shred of defiance he'd ever had from her, ever, and for some reason, it changed everything.

Or perhaps it was only Izar who had changed. Perhaps, he thought with a certain grudging fury at his own failing, he was perverse enough that defiance attracted him. It was, after all, so very rare.

No one defied him. He was Izar Agustin. No one dared.

If Liliana had been any other woman alive, Izar would have handled her much differently. He would have used his hands against her bared, silken flesh. He would have sampled that sulky, insolent mouth and he would have had her on her back on that bed without a moment's pause as he sorted out the variety of ways he disliked being spoken to in that provocative, insulting manner. He would have made her beg and then, when he was good and ready, he'd have made her scream.

*But she was his goddamned ward.*

Izar told himself the tightness in his chest and that raw expanse inside him were more of that unexpected temper, that was all. He focused on the fact this woman, *his ward*, who should have been somewhere far, far away from this grimy little apartment and the ghastly party taking place in all the other small, tatty rooms, was choosing to defy him while dressed like a trollop.

It was insult upon injury, really.

Tonight she'd chosen to wear something that was more a gesture toward a tunic than any kind of dress, baring her arms despite the mid-November cold outside. It flowed from a distractingly low neck to graze her upper thighs, leaving an unnecessary expanse of smooth skin between its hem and her over-the-knee boots. Perfect for a bit of pickup trade, he thought sourly. And perhaps unfairly.

That it was how all young women dressed these days wasn't lost on him. But Liliana wasn't any young woman. She didn't have the option to career about through her early twenties like the rest of them, stacking up questionable evenings and choices and then writing it all off as "experience" once she settled down into a dreary suburban existence somewhere. Her sins would be neither forgiven nor forgotten—

they would be trotted out at every opportunity by tabloids and business rivals alike. She wasn't like all the other, interchangeable girls cluttering up the living areas of this flat.

She was legendary. And she was his.

His *responsibility*, he amended after a moment. A searing, unhelpful moment with nothing but her intoxicating beauty in his head.

"Is this how one dresses here in the toilet of New York City?" he asked edgily, letting his gaze move with cold disapproval from her face to her toes. Then back. "The better to blend in with less-fortunate women on street corners? I must applaud you. How enterprising to attempt to avoid the predators milling about the gutters out there by dressing as if they could simply buy you instead of bothering to go to the trouble of mugging you."

Liliana sucked in a breath. Izar felt something like remorse—another emotion he was largely unfamiliar with, and he certainly didn't care for the experience now—swell in him when her bright gaze dimmed, but she only squared her shoulders. As if she thought she was tough enough to fight him head-on.

Izar didn't care to examine how that notion careened around inside him. The way it left marks.

Liliana frowned at him but didn't break the

way she would have even six months ago. "I'm going to pretend you didn't just call me a prostitute in the first conversation we've had live and in person in a decade."

"I said you appeared to have dressed like one. Is this a costume party? That could certainly explain the number of tarts on parade, yourself included."

She pressed her lips together. He didn't want to think about her lips.

"You're a very small and unhappy man, aren't you, Izar?"

"When confronting my wayward ward in a flat built on lies and a fake name she thinks makes her fireproof and somehow invisible at once?" She finally blinked at that. That belligerent chin of hers dropped a few notches. He was aware that there was no reason these things should have given him quite so much satisfaction, as if he'd scored some kind of decisive victory. "Yes. You could call this unhappiness, if you wish. If I were you, I would be less concerned with my happiness and more concerned with your own hide."

"I'll be really, really scared when I get your letter on the subject three months from now, I promise," she told him after a moment. With deep and unmistakable sarcasm and no apparent recognition of the precariousness of her situation.

"Careful," he warned her, and he hardly recognized his own voice.

She sniffed. "I'm not afraid of you."

"Then you are even more foolish than you appear."

He saw some sort of strong emotion he couldn't quite identify wash over her then, making her stand straighter and cross her arms beneath her breasts which was…not at all helpful.

*She—is—your—ward,* Izar snapped at himself.

What was wrong with him that he couldn't seem to remember that tonight? She and her stake in the company were his responsibility until she turned twenty-five or married, whatever came first. The weight of that had been at the forefront of his thoughts since the day her parents had died. It was why he'd dedicated himself with such ferocity to the business all this time. Why had it deserted him entirely tonight?

But he knew why. It was the way she stood before him, beautiful and wholly unimpressed with him, which was a true novelty. It was that mouthwatering expanse of her thighs, bared for all the world to see. Worse, for *him* to see. It was the sad truth that, apparently, he really was that twisted, after all. That ruined, from the inside out, exactly as he'd always suspected.

"I told you I would bodily remove you from this city the moment you became any kind of scandal," he bit out at her, and it was an effort to keep himself from raising his voice. He didn't entirely succeed. "Congratulations. You lasted longer than I thought you would, but that day has finally arrived."

Liliana frowned. "You told me that when I was eighteen and setting off for college. Newsflash, I survived. The city didn't burn down around me and your precious company is fine. No luxury brands have been harmed by my attempt to have a life, Izar. You can exhale."

Yet another unfamiliar sensation washed over him then, and once more, it took Izar a long moment to recognize it. It had been a while since anyone had gotten under his skin like this. Or at all. Not since his days on the pitch, in fact, where he'd been a bit of a hothead and his opponents had sometimes used that against him. He'd thought he'd locked that side of himself away for good when he'd left the sport.

Why Liliana, of all people, should have the power to needle him when no one else alive could or would dare, Izar could not imagine.

Nor did he care for it.

When he spoke again his voice rivaled the cutting November winds outside.

"You remain my responsibility, whether you like it or not. That means that you cannot live in an unprotected slum like this, no matter how bohemian you currently imagine yourself to be. You are entirely too wealthy for these games."

"I'm not bohemian." She laughed as if he'd told her a joke. "At all."

"On that we agree. It was one thing to hide behind a false name while you were in school. This is not school any longer, Liliana. How long did you really think it would take for someone to discover who you are and use it against you? And let us be clear. When I say *against you*, what I mean is *against the company*, which is the same thing as *against me*."

She shook her head at him as if he was being ridiculous. As if he, Izar Agustin, renowned the world over for his business acumen and corporate vision, was capable of being any such thing.

"I moved in here five months ago and, so far, the only undesirable person to discover me is you."

"That is where you are wrong." He tried to keep the edge out of his voice, but he saw her stiffen. He tried and failed to regret the fact he clearly got to her, too. "Why do you think I am here?"

"Because you live to stamp on dreams and ruin lives, I assume. Mine in particular. You know, the usual."

"Of course." It was amazing how hard it was to hold on to his temper tonight, truly astonishing. "And because I was approached by a piece of tabloid journalist scum who told me he intended to run a vile little article on how I took over the company and consigned the much-adored if seldom-seen Brooks heiress to a life of poverty and toil. Right here in this grimy little hellhole." Izar did nothing to soften his scowl. He didn't even try. "I assured him that was not possible, as no one would describe your parents' perfectly good brownstone in Greenwich Village as *grimy*, much less a hole of any kind. Imagine my surprise to discover that you did not live there, as you had assured me you did following your graduation. In writing. I was forced to track you down. To this place. Which is so much worse than a mere *grimy hole* it defies description."

He didn't know what he expected. But it wasn't for Liliana to do nothing for a moment. Then, after another long moment, blow out a breath and roll her eyes as if what he'd said was…annoying. Nothing more than *annoying*.

He felt his entire body go taut in disbelief.

"The Brooks heiress can go to hell," she announced, and Izar noticed she swayed ever so slightly on her feet as she made this proclamation. He'd thought she'd looked a bit flushed before, hadn't he? "And so can you."

"Liliana." Her name was a grim thing in his mouth. "Are you drunk?"

"Certainly not." She moved across the room and placed the mostly empty wineglass she'd been clutching in one fist on her desktop. With rather more theatric care than was strictly necessary. "I may have had a glass of wine. Like any grown-ass woman over the age of twenty-one in this country, not that it's any of your concern."

"I think you'll find it is, in fact, my concern. As is everything else you do. This is unacceptable, all of this. I trusted you."

"You did not trust me." Her back was an unfortunately fascinating line, graceful and supple and—*stop this. Now.* "You delivered a set of instructions you expected me to obey because I always have before. Your failure to notice that I'm not actually as spineless and obedient as you'd like me to be is your issue, not mine. But that's what happens when you abandon someone for *a decade*."

"Again, it appears I must correct you. My issues are your issues when and if I say they are."

She turned back to face him then, her gaze

dark. "Enjoy yourself while you can, Izar. The clock is ticking. You only have two years left to bully me. What happens when your time runs out?"

He had the urge to put his hands on her and show her exactly what could happen—

But no. Of course he did no such thing. He was her guardian, not an animal. And he hadn't let passion rule him so completely since he was a small boy kicking footballs against crumbling, graffiti-covered walls in his run-down neighborhood, imagining that might transport him out of his dreary life as the unwanted charity case in his resentful uncle's overcrowded home.

He wasn't about to backslide now. Not even for the surprisingly intriguing woman his ward had gone and become without his permission.

"This conversation is over," he informed her, with the expectation of instant obedience. "I'm taking you out of this place at once. I'd suggest you pack a bag now, while I'm feeling generous."

She didn't move. She didn't react at all, in fact, which was far more intriguing than it ought to have been. An alarm went off inside him, deep and low.

"I'm not a grieving twelve-year-old any longer, Izar," she said mildly enough, though her blue eyes flashed. "I'm not going to meekly bow my head and let you toss me away into some mausoleum on a mountaintop because you find my existence troublesome. Not again."

"Will you not?" he asked with soft menace. "Are you quite sure?"

He thought she shivered slightly at that, but if she did she covered it in an instant.

"You control the company. My birthright." Did he imagine the edge in her voice on that last word? He knew he did not imagine the way her eyes flashed at him. "But you no longer control me."

Izar could think of any number of ways to control her—but none of them were the least bit appropriate. He gritted his teeth.

"Careful, Liliana. It is up to me, after all, to determine whether or not your claim to your shares should be honored when you turn twenty-five. If I think you're not up to the challenge of it, I can keep you at arm's length for another five years. Or did you not bother to read the fine print of the birthright you are suddenly so interested in?"

"Is that a threat?" she threw right back at him. "Somehow, I'm not surprised. It doesn't matter. Threaten me all you want. I'm not letting you lock me away in another prison. It's not going to happen."

"Then throw a fit," he invited her. "Like the stroppy child you are so determined to pretend you are not. It will not affect the outcome in any way."

He shrugged as if he didn't care what she did. Because he never had before and he shouldn't now, damn it. He slid his phone out of his pocket and dialed his driver, then lifted the phone to his ear.

Only to watch in sheer astonishment as Liliana closed the distance between them as if she wasn't at all intimidated by him, lifted her slender hand and then *swatted* his mobile out of his grip.

The phone hurtled through the air, making an arc across the quiet bedroom. It seemed to take a lifetime, or perhaps that was simply his disbelief. But then it hit the hardwood floor with a clattering sound and skidded out of sight beneath the bed.

For a moment they both stood there and stared. Her chest rose and fell, threatening the neckline that was already too low for Izar's peace of mind. The color was high on her cheeks and there was something hectic in her gaze, making her eyes entirely too blue. She looked wild, untamed. Golden and gorgeous.

She looked like something straight out of his favorite fantasies.

He was losing his grip.

"That," Izar said distinctly, and through his teeth, "was unwise."

"I want to live here," Liliana told him fiercely, too much passion in her voice, her eyes. And she was much too close to him, besides. "In two years I'll have to take my place at the company the way my parents intended, but until then, I want to be normal. I don't want to live in a fishbowl. I don't want the world commenting on every move I make and every piece of clothing I put on as if it's their business."

She threw up her hands in emphasis or maybe to illustrate how strongly she *felt* these things. God help him, but Izar did not want to *feel*. He did not want to be near anyone who did. Feelings were no good. They led nowhere he wanted to go. He indulged the passions of the flesh because they were easily sated by his ever-revolving selection of mistresses and because he was, after all, a man. But he didn't *feel*. He had sex, then moved on. Passion like this was lethal. He'd excised it a long time ago.

He couldn't remember the last time he'd been so close to someone who fairly *oozed* it.

And she was still speaking. "I want to be a regular person. I want to complain about my job all week, then stand in loud, tacky bars or binge watch television all weekend with my friends. I want the whole experience. Where's the harm in that?"

Some distant voice inside him told him to step back. To remove himself from the temptation of such a ferociously earnest expression on such a beautiful face. The way she tilted her head back so she could stand that close to him and still look him in the eye, as if it was *necessary* she confront him this way. Her faint scent, maddeningly vague, that was somehow a part of the heat of her skin and its softness at the same time, tangling inside of him and making him long for things that were impossible. More than impossible.

He didn't understand how any of this had happened. But he couldn't make this situation any worse than it already was tonight. *He couldn't.*

"I sympathize." He did not touch her. He did not bend his head to taste that full mouth and he did not test the smoothness of her bared arms with his palms. But he also did not back away. "But that is not a choice you have."

"It should be my choice."

"Perhaps. But, instead, it is mine."

"I don't—"

"Do you really think this is wise, Liliana?" he bit out, cutting her off before he stopped remembering why he should. "Do you really think pushing me is going to get you what you want?"

"What will?" she demanded.

And later he might very well rip this moment apart. He might dig through his every motivation and question what the hell he'd been thinking—but here, now, he wasn't sure he thought at all. It was as if she was a cliff when he'd expected a long, flat, familiar meadow, and he'd plummeted straight over the side without any warning. And there was nothing to be done for it now. He should have shut this down and bundled her off into his waiting car the moment she'd walked into the room and confirmed every last thing that smirking cockroach had told him. He shouldn't have engaged with her. He shouldn't have listened to a word she said, because how could it matter? And who cared if the woman who was still his duty had gone and transformed herself into the physical manifestation of his deepest desires? That he noticed at all was appalling. He'd have to add that to his laundry list of reasons to loathe himself. Later.

But in that moment, Izar did more than notice. He let his eyes drift down to her lips and linger there. Almost as if he was powerless to help himself—or stop.

"Oh," she said softly, and the word was ripe with too many meanings. Revelation and understanding. Something like wonder. A touch of daring besides, and it poured through him, molten hot and impossible to resist. "Honey, not vinegar. I should have realized. The great and terrible Izar Agustin only *acts* tough."

She threw herself forward and into him, catching herself with her palms flat against his chest even as his hands came up to grip her upper arms. Automatically, he told himself. To push her away, he told himself—but he didn't.

Her skin was every bit as smooth to the touch as he'd tried not to imagine. The contact was like fire, surging through him, making him insane enough to understand he was hot and hard and unwilling to do a damn thing to change it—

And then Liliana surged up on her toes and pressed her lips to his.

# CHAPTER THREE

KISSING IZAR WAS a great deal like leaping from the top of a high building into an endlessly frozen arctic sea. A giddy rush and then the shock of the cold. The feel of his cruel mouth against hers, his taut chest beneath her hands as if she'd slapped them on a blazing radiator, his hard-packed, solid body too close and too big and too much—

Maybe she had been tipsy before. Because she wasn't now. At all. And she couldn't imagine what in the name of all that was holy she thought she was doing.

For a moment, they stood there as if turned to stone. Liliana's heart kicked at her, hard enough to knock her down, though she didn't let it.

Liliana's whole life seemed to flash before her in an instant. Most of it revolving around the frustrating man whose large, hard hands gripped her upper arms, whose fresh, clean scent was mixed with something dark and spicy that she suspected was all him, and whose mouth was as hard and unyielding as it had looked in all those tabloid photographs.

Her heart walloped her a second time. Harder, maybe.

The wine she'd drunk seemed to spin around inside her, playing back every single word she'd said to her guardian since she'd walked into this room tonight. Liliana shivered. What in the name of God had she been thinking? *Taunting* Izar? Was she mad? He was going to throw her into a dark little cell somewhere and never, ever let her out again, and that would be if she was lucky—

But first she had to deal with the fact that on top of all the things she'd said and the fact she'd attacked him and possibly damaged his mobile phone in the bargain, she'd also thrust herself upon him. She hadn't looked him in the face and now she was *touching* him. She was standing here in her bedroom with her lips attached to his. How would she ever live that down? How could she possibly begin to apologize for such a lapse in judgment?

Her heart kicked at her a third time.

Liliana tensed, ready to push herself away from him and, if there was a God, disappear through the floor or die on the spot as planned—

But Izar made a low, growling sort of noise.

She'd never heard anything like it before, yet it seemed to move through her body, curling around her like smoke. Holding her as tight as he did.

Then he angled his head, hauled her even closer and took control.

And everything exploded.

The world disappeared in the searing flash of it, wild and hot and insane. There was nothing left. No scrap of her at all. There was only the masterful way Izar took her mouth, parting her lips to slip between them and setting her on fire.

He tasted her. He tempted her. He hauled her even closer until she was sprawled against his chest, her breasts flattened against the wall of his torso. And she hardly knew herself, because all she could do was meet him as he pillaged her mouth, winding her arms around his neck and trying to get even closer to him, if that was possible.

There was too much. He was too much. She found her fingers tangling in his crisp, dark hair and could feel even that like a bolt of lightning, searing into her and through her. And she didn't care if she burned alive as long as she could keep doing this. Forever.

He deepened his kiss and she arched against him, understanding when she rubbed against him what that hardness was. She wanted more. She wanted him.

She wanted *everything*.

Because, finally, it all made sense. Her whole life. Her long evenings spent tracking pictures of Izar across the globe, from one glittering party tailor-made for the tabloids to the next. Her tense and painful long-distance relationship with this man and his infrequent letters that had cast such a long and dark shadow over the last decade. It seemed so obvious, suddenly, that everything had been leading here, to the exultation of his mouth on hers, urging her on, making her pant and shiver and think she might die if she couldn't feel the scrape of his marvelous jaw on every part of her skin.

It was as if she'd lived all this time in the dark without ever realizing there was another way, but this kiss threw the door wide open. It let in the light, and the light filled her to bursting.

Izar wrenched his mouth from hers and set her back from him, his black eyes blazing and that arrogant mouth of his she knew the taste of, now, in a grim line. His breathing was uneven, too. Liliana tried to catch her own breath as he muttered something in Spanish, low and harsh. She didn't need to understand the actual words to know it was filthy and likely profane, besides. She could see it in his face.

"This cannot happen," he gritted out.

"It already has," she replied simply.

Izar's hands tightened on her arms—and who knew her *arms* had been an erogenous zone all this time?—and then he dropped them to his side.

"This is unacceptable." He ran a hand over his close-cut black hair, his mouth twisting even as his black eyes glittered with more of that light. She recognized it now. She could feel it inside of her, tearing through dark places she hadn't even known were there. "You are my ward."

"How dirty," Liliana said softly, and she only realized after she'd said it that she was teasing him. She was *teasing* Izar, a man she'd found intimidating when he'd been nothing but autocratic lines on pieces of paper, an email, the occasional text. The world had clearly started spinning in the opposite direction. "How will you bear to look at yourself in the mirror again?"

His mouth flattened. "This is not a joke."

"If you say so. Sir."

He actually growled at her.

And Liliana didn't know what was possessing her tonight. First it had been too much wine, perhaps, though she didn't feel in the least bit buzzy any longer. Not from alcohol, anyway. Who knew what it was now? She only knew that there was magic in her blood and a dark, delicious need she didn't entirely understand, and that she'd never felt anything like this before.

It was him. Maybe it had always been him.

Who wanted to suffer through sloppy kisses from floppy-haired Columbia students when there was this? When there was Izar—a man who was actually, legitimately renowned across the globe for his seduction skills?

And her life was already tangled up with his. It always had been, and no matter that she hadn't been near enough to touch him in a decade. Maybe that was why she wasn't as surprised by this as she should have been. As he clearly was.

"Guardian, ward—what do words matter at this point?" she asked. Reasonably, she thought. "They're just words."

"This is not a debate." He sounded pained. And something far darker than merely furious. His dark eyes glittered. "It's bad enough that any of this occurred. We will not now have a *discussion* about my moral failings, thank you."

"It's not as if you've ever been any kind of father figure to me," she pointed out. She still had no idea where this was coming from, her sudden ability to speak to him as if he was anybody else. To stand up to him, even. "Or any kind of family at all, for that matter. You've gone out of your way to make sure we have little to no actual relationship."

Something that seemed, now, to make a lot of sense. To be necessary, even. In the same way that she now knew how he tasted.

"Get your coat," Izar told her furiously. Or maybe it wasn't fury that made him tense like that, his hands in fists at his side. Maybe it was something more basic, more elemental. Maybe it matched the thing she could feel spiraling around and around inside of her. "It's cold outside."

"Okay," she said obediently, because that was what he expected of her. The instant obedience of a schoolgirl.

But Liliana wasn't a schoolgirl any longer. And there was no point telling Izar that. There was no point making proclamations about the fact she was an adult. She couldn't think of anything more likely to convince him that she was actually still twelve years old, as he clearly believed she was.

Instead of wasting her breath, she reached down to the hem of her tunic, grasped it tight and pulled the whole thing up and over her head. She heard his harsh, indrawn breath as she tossed the filmy thing aside, but she wasn't done. She pulled the pins out of her hair and shook her head, letting it all tumble down around her.

Then she stood there before her guardian in nothing but over-the-knee boots and a tiny little pair of bright teal panties.

Izar looked...tortured. Frozen solid and torn apart at once. That fascinating muscle pulsed in his jaw. His eyes were blacker than she'd ever imagined eyes could be. So black and so bold her nipples pinched into tight, high points.

He made that growling noise again.

"Put your clothes back on. Now." He sounded even more furious than before.

And Liliana didn't know where her courage came from. She didn't understand herself. She only knew that if she did what he asked, if she let this moment pass, she would regret it forever.

She decided she was full up on regrets, thank you. And this was her birthday.

So, instead of obeying him, she moved toward him again.

It was telling that he only watched her come, she thought. That he didn't order her to stop. Not when she was standing in front of him. Not when she leaned closer and then, daring everything, reached down to trace that intriguing hardness behind the fly of his dark trousers with her finger. It made her shiver. *He* made her shiver.

If Izar could have ignited them both with the look in his eyes then, she'd have been reduced to ash. She had no doubt.

But she'd imagined he was larger-than-life for the past ten years. A titan. A fairy tale. Tonight, she'd discovered he was all of that and more. How could she possibly resist?

"Liliana." Her name was an order. But his voice was hoarse. So she used the whole of her palm, testing the shape of him as he pressed like steel against the front of his trousers, and even though he wasn't touching her she felt a hollow sort of restlessness spool out from deep inside of her.

*Hunger*, she thought, as it coursed through her, spiked and greedy. It was pure, unadulterated hunger. For him.

She'd never felt anything like this in her life.

"What about what I want?" She was surprised that her own voice sounded so intense. So needy. But some part of her didn't mind. "What would it hurt if we did that for a change? Just this once? It's my birthday."

Something flared in his dark eyes. He muttered a curse, but then he was fitting his palms to her face as if he couldn't help himself, holding her there where there was no hiding. No pretending. Nothing but naked need.

He studied her face for a long, tense breath,

and Liliana wished she had the slightest notion what he was searching for. What he saw.

"There will be consequences, *gatita*."

"There are always consequences," she whispered. "Who cares?"

His thumbs moved against her cheekbones, so slow and soft she wondered if he was even aware he was doing it. She wasn't certain what was driving her, why she was *so sure*—but he was so hot and so hard beneath her hand and she thought she might die if she didn't get this, at least. One taste. One night. One chance to be like everybody else in the whole world instead of the little freak on her odd little pedestal, untouched and alone.

One chance to be with Izar.

"I will remind you that you said that," Izar growled, and then he took her mouth again.

And Liliana threw herself headfirst into the fire.

If he was going to blow up his life, Izar thought with a certain recklessness he'd never allowed himself in all his days on this earth, why not make it spectacular?

He devoured her. The image of her, his grownup Liliana, standing before him in nothing but that scrap of blue-green silk between her legs and those unreasonable sexy boots, would stay with him to his grave. All that tousled golden hair falling around her to flirt with her dark pink, upturned nipples. Her small, perfect breasts.

If a man was going to fall, why not make sure it was a swan dive?

He gathered her to him, reaching down to pull her hand from the place he was the hardest before he embarrassed himself. And he tasted her. Again and again. He plundered that mouth of hers as if he'd spent his whole life dreaming of nothing but this moment. He hardly knew himself any longer.

But Izar found that with her taste in his mouth and her firm, lean body beneath his hands, he simply didn't care about that the way he should have.

The only thing he could manage to care about just now was making this worse. As bad as possible.

If he was going to do this, he wanted to do it right. He wanted to take her, body and soul. And he didn't particularly want to analyze that notion.

He sat her down on the edge of her neatly made bed and stood looking down at her for a moment, drinking in every moment of this thing that shouldn't have happened and all her shocking, unexpected beauty along with it. God help him, but she was perfect. If he had cobbled together a list of the things he liked most in a woman, he would have come up with Liliana. From her high breasts to the sweet flare of her hips. The long, long legs and that silly little smile on her full mouth, as if she found what was happening between them, this terrible mistake, nothing short of delightful.

It was as if he'd never wanted another woman in his life. As if no one existed or ever had but Liliana.

That notion should have alarmed him. Izar ignored it.

He shrugged out of his coat and tossed it in the vague direction of her desk. It took him mere moments to strip out of the rest of the dark suit he wore and yet it felt like years, as her blue eyes grew darker and got wider with every item he discarded.

"Should…should I take off my boots?" she asked, and the way her voice cracked made him so hard it was almost like an agony. Almost.

"Did I tell you to take off your boots, *gatita*?"

She swallowed hard, then flushed. Bright. Hot.

God help him. This was worse than he'd thought. She was sweet and innocent. He knew this as well as he knew his own name.

But, tonight, she was his.

There were reasons he should have balked at that, but he couldn't think of them just now. There were the consequences he'd mentioned, but he couldn't imagine what those might be any longer. Not while she waited there before him, exquisitely beautiful, her eyes full of him.

Maybe there were men on this earth who could resist her, but Izar was not one of them.

When he was fully naked, he stood there before her and let her look, feeling the way her wide, hungry eyes caressed him like her hands all over his body. And he was arrogant enough to laugh at the way her eyes flew wide when she followed the flat line of his belly down farther. The way her cheeks grew redder still and that stain traveled down her chest to flirt with her lovely breasts.

He no longer cared that this building offended him. That this room reminded him of a prison cell. That he was Izar Agustin and she was Liliana Girard Brooks and if he was truly going to do this thing he shouldn't, there were any number of five-star hotels in Manhattan that would happily fall all over themselves to accommodate him and let him handle this moment in a setting far more appropriate for them both.

But she was near enough to naked, with her heart in her eyes. And he found that after all the thousands of ways he'd been ruined almost before he'd started and had imagined himself untouchable because of it, he was more susceptible to that—to her—than he ever would have dreamed possible.

Izar stopped thinking, assuming he'd done any of that since she'd walked into this room and stolen his sanity. He stopped questioning.

There was no point thinking about it any longer.

There was only now. There was only this.

Izar crossed back to her bed. He took his ward in his arms, and he proceeded to lose himself entirely.

He didn't care.

There was only Liliana, and no matter if it burned them both.

Izar was like a fury, hard and hot and relentless.

Liliana loved it.

He spread her out before him on the bed and then he crawled over her, and Liliana thought it was too much. That it alone might kill her. That her heart couldn't possibly stay where it belonged, inside her chest, when it catapulted against her ribs in such a tumult.

*He was so big.* He braced himself over her and gazed down at her, and Liliana thought she'd never felt so trapped in her life. Except this trap, she liked. More than liked. He was smooth and muscled, and while photographs had always celebrated the man's physicality, *this* was a whole new way of appreciating it. Him. The wall of his chest was ridged and mouthwatering, and she wanted to rub her face against his skin and lose herself in that hollow between his flat, hard pectoral muscles.

She wanted a thousand things she was afraid to name, that she'd only dared imagine when she was buried under the covers with pictures of him dancing in her head, alone.

But then he began to kiss her. He took her mouth again, with a certain ruthless laziness that left her boneless beneath him, clutching his big biceps to anchor her to the earth. Izar left her mouth, laughing when she made a soft noise of protest, and he lavished that same attention on her jaw, her neck. He traced his way down one side of her collarbone and up the other. He seemed to have all the time in the world, and who cared if she writhed or moaned or called out his name?

If anything, he went slower.

He found one breast and he learned it. His lips, his tongue, his hard and clever hands. The faint, teasing edge of his teeth. He made her shake. He lit her on fire. And only when she was gripping his hair as if she might want to pull it out did he relent.

And then move to the other one, making it perfectly clear he would do with her body exactly as he wished.

Liliana lost all sense of time, of place. There was nothing left in the whole of the universe save the dark, beautiful man who sprawled there above her and made her body into his playground. He laid a trail of fire down the center of her body, his wicked hands following along with that endlessly inventive mouth of his, tying her into knots and then pulling them tight. Then tighter. Then tighter still.

She couldn't breathe, and he was only toying with her navel. She was dying—but he paid her gasps and her deep, long shudder no mind at all as he moved between her legs. He propped them open with his wide shoulders, the suede of her boots rubbing against his bare skin, and it was all somehow almost hotter than she could bear.

Liliana didn't live in a cave. She knew what he was about to do. She'd dreamed of it.

But nothing could have prepared her for Izar. The shockingly male reality of him. That blaze of fire burning in his dark eyes as he looked up at her. That faint curve to his stern, uncompromising mouth. That relentless, rampant masculinity of his that made her feel deliciously, eternally soft and hot and his.

He toyed with her. He reached down and traced her swollen core with a lazy finger, through the lacy fabric of her panties.

And Liliana toppled off the edge of everything she knew, into pure sensation. He played with her, drawing lazy patterns as he liked and then slipping beneath the bright scrap of lace to test the core of her. She couldn't handle it and yet she wanted—needed—more. Fire charged through her, setting her alight and making her shiver uncontrollably. She bucked against his hand and moaned out loud when he held her in place.

"Please." She barely recognized her own voice, choked with hunger. *"Please."*

*"Gatita."* His voice was stern. "I cannot imagine I have ever given you the impression that I take direction well."

He took his time. He played with her soft, wet heat until she was near enough to mindless, thrashing beneath him. And when he was ready, and only then, he sank one long, hard finger deep inside her where no one had ever gone. No one. Ever.

Izar muttered something in harsh, rich Spanish, and when he pulled his hand away, Liliana cried out. She couldn't help herself.

"I know," he told her, his voice low and sure, and she believed him. "I know."

And then he leaned down, held her panties to one side and licked his way into her core.

Liliana fractured. She splintered into a thousand shards of herself, and still he kept on. He tasted her. He tormented her. He slid that finger back inside her as he toyed with her, thrusting in and out of her body as he used that marvelous mouth of his against her. Everything inside her pulled into a taut, hard, red knot as she arched into him, utterly lost to his touch.

And then she really did shatter. Again and again and again.

Maybe she even screamed.

When she came back to herself she was hoarse and he was sitting up, tugging her boots from her legs and tossing them to the bedroom floor. Then he reached up and pulled her panties down her legs.

And she could do nothing but lie there and watch him do as he liked with her, mesmerized by his stark male beauty and all that wild shattering still swirling around and around inside of her.

He crawled back over her, gathering her beneath him again, and the fact he was still so blazingly hot made her sigh in renewed pleasure. He settled himself against her, cradling her face in his hands as, below, the hard heat of him nudged against her. She was so soft, so wet, it made her flush with embarrassment, but he only smiled.

"Courage, *gatita*," he told her. "It will only hurt a moment."

"Why do you keep calling me that?" she asked, in that same half-strangled voice, making her wonder if she really had screamed. And why she couldn't seem to care about that the way she might have only hours earlier. "Little cat?"

"I had no idea you had claws," he told her, and there was a curve to his hard mouth that made her think he meant to be gentle. Yet the look in his dark eyes was intent. It was like a whole new shattering. "I find I like it."

"Izar…" she whispered.

But that was when he thrust inside her.

She expected it to hurt, and not only because he'd said it would. But because that was always the story. It was supposed to be traumatic. Agonizing, searing, ripping her open—

"Are you scowling at me because you're in pain?" he asked mildly, as if he wasn't lodged deep inside of her. Naked and *inside* her.

That made her frown deepen. "No," she said. "Because I'm not."

"If it doesn't hurt, Liliana, then perhaps you might consider not scowling at all."

"It's supposed to hurt. It's supposed to be terrible." She blew out a frustrated breath and experimented with the *oddness* of it, that a part of his body was deep inside her. That he was so *close*. That this was happening and it wasn't at all the way she'd imagined it would be. "It's how you know you're a woman."

"That is not how you know you are a woman, I fervently hope."

"Forgive me if I don't take your word on that," she retorted drily. "Given you lack the proper equipment to make that—"

But that was when he moved.

It was a lazy slide out, then back. Hardly more than a little shift of his hips.

Heat bloomed…everywhere. Nerve endings she didn't know she had burst to life, and she rocked against him, wanting…more. Less. Again. *Everything*.

Izar leaned down and pressed his lips to that furrowed space between her eyes.

"Stop frowning," he ordered her, but his voice was softer than she'd imagined it could ever be and that, too, shuddered through her. "It will not hurt you to let yourself enjoy the things for which I do, in fact, possess the proper equipment."

It made her feel new. Vulnerable and safe at once, and that was before he pulled back and she could see the look on his forbidding face. Not soft. But still, not the ferocious, big bad wolf Izar of her imagination. There was a light in his black eyes that made her feel as if this might be his version of *tender*.

"It's okay," she said quietly. "I forgive you for not hurting me." She waited a moment. Deliberately. "Sir."

A strange expression moved over him then, as if he couldn't quite puzzle her out, but then it was gone. And then he smiled.

And Liliana didn't have the words to describe how that felt. What it did. How it poured over her and through her and became part of what was happening, somehow. That impossible hardness inside of her and a smile on the face of this man who had ruled over her whole life, beaming into her as if he was his own source of light.

"I appreciate that," he said solemnly, but there was a faint curve to his hard mouth and that gleam in his dark black eyes. "Now hold on."

And he didn't wait for her to obey. He started to move.

This time, he didn't stop. He rocked into her, setting an easy pace and watching her as she learned how to meet him. How to move with him to make those wild, incandescent sensations better. Wilder. Hotter.

God, it was so hot it should have killed them both. Maybe it did.

He moved faster then. He dropped his head to hers and he took her mouth again, taking her everywhere. Making her his as surely as if he'd branded her, and Liliana thrilled to the thought.

She'd asked for *this once* and he was giving it to her, this man who had gone out of his way to give her so little before. And so here, on this bed, in this stark little room she hadn't realized she'd made into a cell, she didn't hide a thing. She poured herself into this dance of bodies, this mad tango that stunned her and inspired her with every deep, thrilling stroke.

All the complicated feelings he'd stirred in her from afar all these years, which she'd cobbled together and called *hate* because it was easier. All the need and longing inside of her she'd never understood she was saving for him.

For this.

Liliana had waited her whole life for this, for him, for Izar.

And it was even better than she'd dared imagine.

He slid his hands beneath her, lifting her hips to his, and then he increased his pace. He murmured words she didn't understand, wrapping them in a cloak of fervent Spanish and his masterful touch.

And when that huge fist of sensation centered

in the core of her, it terrified her. She didn't think she'd survive it.

"I can't," she whispered—or maybe she screamed it. She couldn't tell the difference any longer.

"I insist," he murmured against the tender skin of her neck.

And he gave her no choice but to obey.

On his next deep thrust she broke into a thousand pieces, bright red and made of fire, falling all around them and soaring straight over the side of the world. At last.

And the last thing she remembered before she lost herself in all that sensation was the way he called out her name as he followed.

## CHAPTER FOUR

WHEN LILIANA CAME back to herself, Izar was already up and dressed and back to standing forbiddingly in front of her windows. He'd even retrieved his mobile from beneath the bed and was typing into it, frowning faintly as he stared down at the device in his hands.

He looked...exactly the same as he looked in all those pictures she'd studied so closely. Deeply forbidding and faintly inconvenienced. Completely remote. A dark-haired, black-eyed devil with the most arrogant mouth she'd ever seen in her life. Only the fact that Liliana was naked convinced her that she hadn't simply fallen, hit her head and imagined everything that had gone on between them over the course of this unexpected evening.

She told herself she didn't mind that, despite the fact it had clearly happened, that she obviously hadn't had a delusional episode, Izar had reverted to his usual chilly type. If he could have disappeared entirely and left a brutally short and brisk letter in his place, she was sure he would have.

In truth, she was surprised he hadn't.

But getting straight back to reality was a good thing, surely. It was only a few inconvenient expectations that were gnawing at her and making this seem more fraught than it should. That was on her, she told herself sternly. She should never have allowed any sort of silly expectations to enter into…whatever this was…in the first place. Nothing on this earth mattered less than the fact she knew, now, what it was like to stand in a room with him. How he held himself, all finely honed grace and ruthless power, leashed in the finest clothes possible. How his mouth felt all over her skin. And what it was like when he thrust inside of her.

Still, there was a hollow space in her chest even as she thought these things, and rubbing it with her hand did nothing to make it feel any better.

It took her a moment to sit up, but she did. Gingerly. She could feel parts of herself she wasn't used to feeling quite so vividly, but nothing *hurt*. She was wrecked and altered forever, inside and out, but no matter. At least nothing *hurt*. And she was like everybody else now, just as she'd always wanted. No longer the odd one out, in this at least.

Liliana told herself she was lucky. For once in her life she'd gotten exactly what she'd wanted from Izar. She should have been happy.

She told herself that's exactly what she was.

But the brazen, carefree creature she'd been playing all night seemed to have deserted her, and Liliana was very much her usual self as she reached down toward the foot of the bed for the quilt. The better to hide herself away before she died of embarrassment, lying here naked and exposed in front of her fully clothed guardian.

He must have heard her move, because he glanced up and caught her gaze. She froze, not wanting him to see her cover herself, because surely that would tell him all sorts of things she didn't want him to know. But not covering herself meant she was…uncovered.

And he was Izar.

Liliana was sure she turned even more hues of scalding red, because she could feel the way she flushed and how her skin felt tight and itchy. Everywhere. Izar, by contrast, could have been a field of freshly fallen snow for all the discomfort he showed. If he felt anything at all—and despite what she'd been so sure of when they'd been locked together on this bed, Liliana had no idea if that had been nothing more than her own wishful thinking—it didn't show.

"Get dressed," he said.

She'd spent a decade parsing every word he said in interviews. His inflection, his tone, the look in his eyes as he said it. Liliana had long considered herself something of an expert when it came to reading him. She'd been sure she could see when he was amused, impatient— all while he stood and let the press have their way with him.

But tonight she got nothing. He was entirely neutral—or entirely shut down and self-contained. She couldn't read his darkly handsome face one way or another, and that hollow thing inside her seemed to yawn wider. It was hard to imagine this was the same man who had just surrendered to the same passion she had. If she hadn't been there herself, she'd have been certain it wasn't possible.

"I thought maybe I'd take a nice warm bath," she managed to say. Compared to earlier, she was sure she sounded subdued. Well, there was no helping that. "But thank you."

"Not that thing you were wearing earlier," he continued as if she hadn't spoken. The very physical manifestation of his dismissive, condescending letters over the years. *You are too young for Paris.* Or, *There is no reason at all for the Brooks heiress to immerse herself in unnecessary theater courses.* "Something more suitable for a woman of your station, I think."

Liliana didn't want to do what he asked, purely to spite him. But cowering on her bed, naked and at his mercy, was also less than appealing. She gritted her teeth and she climbed out of the bed. She wanted to snap something at him, throw something, say something cutting about his bedside manner—but refrained. He would reply, in all likelihood. That was the trouble. All the fights she'd had with him before tonight had been entirely in her head.

And losing her virginity might not have hurt the way Madame had always direly promised it would, but Liliana had no doubt whatsoever that if Izar wanted, he could tear her apart with a few words. She contented herself with wild fantasies of a variety of painful ways to rend him to pieces as he simply stood there, eyes on his phone, while she moved past him with as much dignity as she could muster.

*Stark naked.*

Honesty compelled her to admit, if only to herself, that she didn't know if she was more stung by the fact that he was ordering her around as if nothing had changed between them tonight—or the fact he was apparently perfectly content to ignore her while he did it.

Her closet wasn't so much a walk-in as it was half-empty, so she stepped inside it as best she could and pretended it was a separate, private dressing room. She let her gaze move over her careful collection of wardrobe staples, trying to decide what Izar meant when he said *suitable*. There was a part of her that seriously considered throwing on a bikini and a pair of absurd heels for the pure joy of messing with him, but she thought better of it in the next instant. She'd pushed enough boundaries for one night. Heaven help her if he pushed back.

Liliana pulled on a much-beloved pair of upscale corduroys, the fine-gauge wales buttery soft to the touch, her favorite sweater that also happened to be a quiet sort of classic that was as easily worn at church as out to dinner, and a far more sensible pair of knee-high boots than the ones she'd been wearing. She twisted her hair out of her way and knotted it at the nape of her neck without having to glance in a mirror, one of the more useful skills she'd learned in boarding school. It was a favorite casual work outfit, and just like that she looked pulled together. It was as *suitable* as she could get when all she really wanted was to sink into a very hot bath and process what the hell had happened here tonight.

Here. Inside her. *To* her.

*With him.*

When she stepped back into the bedroom, Izar had put his phone away and was watching her. With an intent, dark focus that made something inside of her twist into a knot, then shiver. Liliana had wanted that only moments before, yet now she thought she might have preferred it if he'd continued to ignore her.

His eyes were too black. An inky midnight with that glitter she still couldn't read though it made her feel soft and hot all over again.

Worse, she thought he could tell.

"Satisfied?" she asked as brusquely as possible, to divert attention from the red in her cheeks. She held her arms out from her sides, trying to channel the crazy person who had inhabited her body earlier and thrown herself at him. Images and remembered sensations threatened to pour over her, but she fought them back. It was that or crawl into a ball in the corner and stay that way for an ice age or two, and she doubted he'd let that happen. "Do I pass the mysterious Izar Agustin prostitute test?"

"The test has nothing to do with me." His voice was such a dark confection. Her body thrilled to it. Something turned over, deep inside her, and pulsed. "It is about you. Who you are, not who I am."

"Maybe I want the Brooks heiress to be

known for her daring fashion choices." She shook her head at him, hoping she looked more certain of that than she felt. "Or for failing to make any *fashion choices* at all, and simply walking around in regular clothes like anyone else."

"But I do not," Izar said quietly. When she glared at him, he shifted slightly, then sighed. And there was no reason she should have felt that like some kind of tiny victory when she didn't even know what it meant. His gaze was level. Steady. "You own half of some of the finest couture houses in the world. Your name is synonymous with luxury. Your taste must necessarily be widely regarded as impeccable. That means there is no room for childish flirtations with the execrable trends your collegiate friends think are fashionable. You do not follow trends, *gatita*. You cannot. You are Liliana Girard Brooks, and you must set them." He nodded toward the door before she could process that. Any of that. "And it is time for us to go."

Momentum and habit had her through the door and into Kay's bedroom before she knew what she was doing. Liliana checked her roommate's bed as a reflex and was relieved to find it empty, for once. But she stopped dead on the far side of the small room and turned back to face him.

"Wait. Where exactly are we going?"

*"Date prisa,"* he muttered impatiently, and clearly not to her. He reached past her and pushed open the next door, then guided her through it with a not precisely gentle hand in the small of her back. "I am not going to stand in a stranger's bedroom in this appalling flat discussing my plans or my agenda, thank you."

She let him move her through Jules's darkened room, where snores from the bed suggested all sorts of things that she was certain Izar would take the wrong way. Sure enough, the look he slanted down at her as they stepped out into the living room was condemning. To put it mildly.

"These are the people you choose to live with?" he asked, his voice as scathing as that look. "This is the life you want for yourself?"

She might not have felt particularly bold in the aftermath of…whatever that had been. But it was one thing to snipe at her. Liliana could take that on the chin if necessary. What she refused to tolerate was listening to him cast his nasty aspersions on her friends.

"Are you about to make one of your snide little comments about virtue, Izar?" she asked him. "Aren't you afraid your hypocrisy will choke you if you dare?" She waited that simmering, deliberate beat. *"Sir?"*

Izar went very still, in a manner that made her think of dark forests and the predatory things that lived there, lurking. His face was like a blade in the shadows of this far corner of the living room. A very sharp, very lethal blade—but she didn't back down. She couldn't, no matter how little her wobbly knees seemed to want to challenge him. She might dress as he dictated and follow his orders by rote, but she couldn't let him insult her friends. She simply *couldn't*.

"Get your coat, Liliana," he said. Very quietly yet with utter authority. She felt it move inside of her, as if his words were tipped in iron. "We are leaving this place. Now."

Liliana stared back at him. She heard the television from the main part of the living room, something involving grand explosions. And there were a few voices farther away, as if there were still people gathered in the kitchen the way there always were at parties. And she'd certainly heard that note of finality in Izar's voice.

"You can't actually force me to leave with you," she pointed out.

Unwisely.

An unholy light flared in Izar's dark gaze then, slamming into her even as he reached across the distance that separated them and took her chin in his hand. Not in any kind of hard or bruising grip, but not exactly gently, either. She didn't know what was more overwhelming, that light in the darkness of his eyes or the definitive way his hand curled around her jaw. Or maybe the fact her body didn't seem to care how he touched her, so long as he did, and hummed.

She understood that humming now. That prickling sensation. She knew exactly what it meant.

"Listen to me very carefully, Liliana," Izar said, each word like a bullet. "I am not playing these games with you. You are mine."

She didn't react to that. Of course she didn't react to that. It didn't burst open inside her and make her feel…a bright many things she had no intention of naming. It certainly didn't make her tremble—helpless and needy and despite herself—which he could almost certainly feel as his hand gripped her chin, forcing her to keep her eyes on his.

And Izar wasn't finished. "And nothing of mine is staying in this hovel. I do not care at all how you leave this dire place. I'll carry you out kicking and screaming if I must."

Liliana wanted to divert his attention from her silly reaction to him, to what he'd said. To *you are mine*, which he likely meant the way he meant it about, say, his cars. His famous collection of astoundingly expensive timepieces too artisanal to be called mere watches. His scattered investment properties in every gorgeous corner of the world, from the untouched sands of far-off Pacific Islands to high in the mighty European Alps. Not…how it had sounded.

Possessive. Hungry.

"They'll stop you," she warned him.

"Who will?" Izar's voice was scornful. "These drunken children at the end of yet another run-of-the-mill debaucherous evening? I doubt that very much, even if they could stand." His grip on her chin tightened. "The choice is yours. Walk out with some measure of dignity or go out over my shoulder like a child in the midst of a tantrum. I do not particularly care which you choose. The outcome will be the same either way."

She didn't know how she kept herself from shaking even harder then. How she kept the emotion that threatened to swamp her from spilling out in tears, which would shame her beyond reason. Or how she managed to meet and hold that lethal glare of his.

"I want to know where we're going," she managed to say, and she thought she almost sounded in control—

But then his hard mouth curved, and she realized belatedly that the question itself implied the surrender she hadn't quite meant to hand over so easily. If at all.

"I want a great many things," he told her, and Liliana could hear the very male, very stark triumph in his voice. She could see it on the face she knew, somehow, she'd never again think was anything but beautiful no matter how overbearing or awful he was, and it was the same as handing him a weapon.

"Life is unfair, *gatita*." It was as if Izar read her mind. He let go of her and jutted his strong chin in the direction of the front door, and that look on his hard face dared her to challenge him. "Start walking or prepare to be hauled out of here. Now."

Izar didn't give his ward time to stage any more protest scenes, however ineffectual. The moment she made her choice and started walking toward the door, stiff legged and clearly furious as she grabbed her coat from the line of pegs on the wall, he hurried her out of that ghastly apartment and into the decidedly sketchy stairwell, which was an improvement only because it meant they were leaving. No time for goodbyes to the drunken idiots who remained, splayed out on the couches and the sticky floor. No chance for any second thoughts.

By the time they made it to street level, his initial fury was back and at the boiling point.

He told himself it was about the fact she'd

lived in such an unsafe place. That she'd lied to him. That she seemed to have absolutely no sense of who she was and her place in this world and had made herself a target for a worm of a paparazzo.

"I suggest you refrain from speaking to me until we are out of this neighborhood and I can forget it exists," he growled at her when they were finally safely in the back of his waiting car and speeding away from this benighted place.

She should have been grateful, of course. The twelve-year-old he'd been imagining all this time would have been, he was sure of it. *This* Liliana shot him a look that suggested all kinds of insulting things, none of them her gratitude. She sat on the whisper-soft seat next to him, close enough that her scent was in his head and driving him mad all over again, and scowled. At him.

"I don't think you're doing a very good job."

"As your guardian? I could not agree more."

"That's not what I meant."

Izar shrugged. "There are always consequences. I feel certain I mentioned that."

What he was certain of was that no one in his entire life had ever looked at him the way she did then. As if he was a crashing bore and she was barely able to tolerate his presence. He, who routinely declined the naked invitations of crowds of stunning women wherever he went. He, who was regularly hailed as one of the most eligible bachelors in the entire world. He could click his fingers together in any country on earth and have battalions of women and men alike prostrate before him, desperate to do his bidding, yet this little twenty-three-year-old who'd spent her life locked away in convent-like boarding schools and women's colleges found him tiresome. It was so outrageous it was almost funny.

Almost.

"You should have mentioned that these consequences would involve racing around the freezing cold city late in the night when all I wanted was a warm bath," she told him in a tone he could hardly fail to notice was completely devoid of any respect. "I thought you meant, you know, a tedious lecture on my vague responsibilities you might or might not allow me to take on one day. Not torture."

And everything was different now. Izar's hands itched to grab her and haul her into his lap, the better to teach her the sort of object lessons he craved to impart in this particular mood—but he had to play this correctly. If he knew anything about his ward, it was that she was far more bloody-minded and stubborn than she should have been. That ramshackle apartment was proof. How she'd lowered herself to live in such a place when she didn't have to he would never know—but the fact she had meant he had to carefully ease her into a new future.

Because he'd planned it all out. The single course of action available to him, having betrayed himself and his responsibilities so spectacularly, had come to him in a rush while he'd still been in her bed.

The truth was that Izar Agustin could not *date* the Brooks heiress, known the world over to be his ward. He should never have slept with her, but having done so, he could not ignore it. He could not have any kind of casual relationship with the woman who owned half his company and would run it with him, as an equal, in two short years.

He'd touched her. He'd taken her. He'd claimed her innocence.

This meant he would have to keep her. Marry her. Make her his in every conceivable way, forever. There was no *just this once*, no so-called birthday gifts, no playing around with the future he'd dedicated his whole life to preserving for her. There was no going back from this epically bad decision.

It almost amused him that of all the many women in the world who would have swooned with glee at the very notion of marrying him, he'd located the only one he knew who would definitely not have that reaction when he told her the good news. Quite the opposite, in fact. But he had always done what was best for her. Whatever else might have changed tonight, that had not.

So he didn't tell her.

He didn't respond to her deliberate provocation. He didn't engage. He ignored her the way he always had before this night that he refused to view as catastrophic. It was a change, certainly. It might cause some comment when it became public, but when had he not caused comment? He was Izar Agustin. He'd decided this sudden shift in their relationship was an opportunity, and so it would prove.

Izar sat back in his appropriately well-appointed car and let his driver whisk them off toward the private airfield where his plane waited. He fired off emails to his staff as his bride-to-be sat beside him, quite obviously fuming into the night. He would have every last trace of her removed from that apartment before dawn, as if she'd never set foot in the Bronx at all, which would make it difficult to take the pictures necessary for a truly damaging tabloid exposé. He would erase this entire chapter of her life. And by the time she really understood what was happening, he intended to be on a plane and far away, when it would be far too late for her to do anything about it.

"We had sex," she said some time later, because this new Liliana was nothing if not constitutionally incapable of doing as he wished.

"In case you wondered," he replied without looking up from his mobile, "I greatly prefer it when you are docile, obedient and quiet. I could do without this provoking, ill-mannered creature you've treated me to tonight."

She let out a crack of laughter that he felt in his sex, like her hands wrapped around him again.

"The provoking, ill-mannered creature is *why* we had sex," she pointed out, but her voice wasn't brazen and carefree the way it had been in her bedroom. There was something else beneath it, hollow and charged at once, that he refused to let scrape at him. *He refused.* "To the best of my recollection. *You* didn't kiss *me*."

Izar put down his phone and met her gaze. It cost him to keep his cool, but he'd learned that trick long ago in far more difficult circumstances than these. To at least appear unbothered on the surface when below he was…volcanic.

He couldn't say he liked the fact that she brought these old ghosts out in him. But now that he knew she could, surely he'd be better prepared. Surely he could keep her from doing any actual damage. He might have succumbed to a hunger he hadn't known he possessed tonight. He might have been walloped by passion—something he hadn't believed could happen to him, ever—and he might have done something he'd have imagined was inconceivable only hours before. But he wasn't going to be taken by surprise again.

Izar had lost his control this once. Only this once.

Once was enough.

"What is it you want?" he asked, razor sharp and ice-cold.

She blinked. "I don't want anything. I just… We had sex. *We. Had sex.*" She looked away again, back out toward the road speeding past them in the dark. "I realize that's something you do a bit more than some, of course. All those busty women who complain in the magazines about your roving eye and so on. So maybe you didn't notice what happened tonight, but I did."

Izar had been so sure that the night couldn't surprise him any further. That she couldn't. But he was all too able to identify what he felt then, far worse than any old ghosts of his hotheaded youth. It was a dark ribbon of shame, wrapping around him and pulling tight down deep in his gut. Reminding him that whatever else she was, whatever had to happen next between them, Liliana had been an innocent tonight. And she had given herself to him.

She was his and she didn't even know it.

Izar gave in to an urge he hadn't known he had and wouldn't have indulged if he'd thought about it further. He reached over and lifted her, hauling her out of her seat and settling her across his lap. She let out a soft, surprised little sound that raced through his blood and heated it. Then she settled herself against him, and that was an exquisite bit of torture he knew he deserved. She was soft in his arms and her bottom was taut and pressed tight against his lap. She slid her arms around his neck, her gaze solemn in the mix of light and shadow that fell into the back of the car as they raced through the city.

Izar indulged himself. He pulled her closer, holding her where he wanted her so he could taste that mouth of hers again. And again. But a simple taste wasn't enough, not now he'd had her, and so he drank a little deeper, took a little more—

But he didn't want to take her in the backseat of a car. Not when he'd taken her virginity in the first place in a grotty old flat. What was happening to him that he would even consider it?

He couldn't remember the last time he'd been

so close to losing control at all, much less twice in an evening. And he couldn't have that. He refused to let anyone have that kind of power over him.

But, first, he made his kiss his penance. He owed Liliana at least that much. He let her tremble against him and squirm maddeningly in his lap. He kissed her as if they had all the time in the world, as if there was nothing but the drag of his lips against hers, the touch of their tongues, the sweet burn of her mouth against his.

He kissed her the way he should have earlier. The way a good man might have kissed an innocent. The way a beautiful woman deserved to be kissed, in celebration of her. An act of reverence.

Again and again he tasted her, until he lost track of where he ended and she began. There was nothing but sensation and need and the perfection that was her mouth open beneath his, her soft body in his arms, her need and wonder like a new perfume, surrounding them.

He could have kissed her all night. He thought perhaps he did.

She was breathing hard when he let her go. When he ordered himself to let her go, because the other option was to lose himself inside her again. Here, in the back of a car, like an appalling American pop song. As if he was a man with no restraint, no self-control. Outside the car windows, he could see that they'd left the city behind and had made it out into the western suburbs of the city, which meant they were getting close to the airfield.

What was happening to him? That he should need an external reprieve—that the iron will he had cultivated and made his defining characteristic was no longer sufficient?

"I noticed, Liliana," he told her gruffly, running his thumb over her impossibly carnal mouth, damp from his. He'd noticed her, first and foremost. He'd certainly noticed they'd had sex. And he'd noticed that somehow, in the middle of all that, his unexpectedly lovely ward had developed a power over him he could never, ever let her know she had. "Believe me."

Her cheeks reddened again, and he slid her back into her own seat before he gave in to temptation and let the part of him that ached for her the most do his thinking for him. He stared down at his mobile, but he didn't see a single thing on his screen. Her taste was in his mouth. His hands *hurt* with the need to touch her again.

He was so deeply in trouble here he hardly knew what to make of it.

But the miles ticked by in the late-fall night, and beside him, Liliana was still. She stared out the windows at the passing lights on the highway, but she didn't appear to see it any more than he'd been capable of reading his messages. He told himself that was just as well. That this was the Liliana he'd imagined all these years. Quiet, self-effacing. Obedient.

This was the Liliana he wanted as his wife.

Whatever had gotten into her tonight was the aberration, he was certain. And while he couldn't quite regret that as he should, Izar refused to resign himself to a fractious married life with some strident termagant simply because it might make good business sense. He wouldn't, come to that. He could chalk up her uncharacteristic behavior to too much wine and far too much unchecked freedom, something Liliana was unlikely to experience again if he had anything to say about it.

And he did.

The benefits of his marrying the Brooks heiress far outweighed any potential ethical questions about his guardianship. Marrying his former partners' daughter made financial sense, pure and simple. It would consolidate all the company's power in their marriage—and, more to the point, in his own two hands—and leave no openings for anyone else to get in there and cause trouble.

He assured himself there was absolutely no

reason he couldn't treat her as he always had, with the added benefit of access to her succulent body. Liliana would make him a lovely wife. Izar was not pedigreed in any sense, but he was so wealthy it made people forget that he'd come from less than nothing and had made every last cent at his disposal. Liliana, meanwhile, was blue-blooded enough for the pair of them, dating back a century or two on both sides. Moreover, she would look like a rare gemstone on his arm, polished and gleaming, and their business was one of lavish appearances and exquisite taste on display. He'd meant what he'd told her earlier. She was the heiress to a very particular, very chic and elegant throne. She needed to look the part. Together they would look like an old-school power couple, all understated, high-class elegance. Now that he was allowing himself to consider it, he couldn't think of anything that would move more product than a high-couture fairy-tale wedding, decked out in the diamonds, gowns and to-die-for clothes and accessories that made Agustin Brooks Girard the institution it was.

Izar didn't understand why he hadn't thought of this before, and much more seriously.

He was congratulating himself on his ability to make colossal mistakes that were actually strokes of brilliance in disguise as the car made it to the airfield at last and drove straight out onto the tarmac. He climbed out, enjoying the slap of the cold air against his face. Then he reached in and pulled Liliana out behind him, delivering instructions to his driver in rapid-fire Spanish as she stood there beside him, looking around in confusion as if she'd never seen a private airfield before.

"Come," he said, and the sound of his voice made her start. She blinked at him as if she'd never seen him before, either.

Izar took her hand and started toward the plane, and he had almost begun to imagine she would simply obey him the way he'd like when he felt her pull against his hand and slow down.

He could have dragged her. But the fact he even considered doing so appalled him and made him stop walking at once. He was not going to *drag* Liliana onto this plane. She was going to board it of her own free will.

Or, at least, she would do so because he wished it.

"You look overwhelmed," he said calmly, a bit coolly, his gaze searching hers. "I feel certain this is not the first time you have seen an airplane, Liliana."

She looked fragile. That was what was getting beneath his skin, out here in the cold with the November wind cutting through him. He wanted to bundle her up and carry her off somewhere where nothing could threaten her again, not even him.

And he had no idea where such an absurd thought came from.

"Where are we going?" Liliana pressed her lips together as if they were dry. He should not have wanted to taste them to find out. "Are you dragging me off to another prison in the middle of nowhere?"

"Saint Moritz," he told her. "Not quite the middle of nowhere and certainly not a prison." He had a very private villa in the hills outside the world-famous ski resort high in the Swiss Alps, though the season wasn't due to start for another week or so. "You know how to ski, do you not? I thought it was one of the numerous ways your boarding school prepared you for its very narrow, remarkably well-heeled version of life."

"I haven't skied since I was a teenager," she said, frowning, but when he tugged her along with him she kept walking, and there was no reason he should feel that like a victory. "And I can't go off to Saint Moritz for the weekend. I have things to do here."

Izar didn't correct her impression that she was going away for a mere weekend. The aide who traveled with him had stayed behind at her apartment to initiate the emptying of it and would arrive shortly with all of Liliana's necessary documents. She could figure out she wasn't coming back at her leisure—in Switzerland, perhaps, when there was even less to be done about it than there was here.

"It is your birthday, Liliana," he reminded her. "Surely you can be forgiven an indulgence or two."

She frowned up at him again as they approached the folded-down stairs that stretched from the plane to the tarmac. She paused at the foot, but then she blew out a breath into the night and Izar told himself that feeling rushing through him was not *relief* as she moved forward. There was no reason his chest should feel so tight, as if he was personally invested in this. In what she did or how she did it. As if it was something more than good sense and good business.

As if the truth was not in the decisions he'd made, but about that flash of fire and the thoughtless tumble he'd taken deep into the heart of it.

Liliana climbed up the stairs and he followed, ushering her into the plane's lavish cabin that better resembled a very high-end hotel suite. There was no reason she should look around as if she had never been on a plane before.

And even less reason that her obvious fragility should…*gnaw* at him.

She sat down on one of the couches with a certain preciseness to her movements that set off alarms inside of Izar. He tensed where he stood, watching her smooth her hands down her thighs as if gathering strength from her markedly well-made corduroys.

And when Liliana looked at him this time, her blue eyes were uncomfortably clear.

"Why are you pretending to care about me?" she asked. Very calmly. "It's starting to unnerve me."

"I beg your pardon?"

"Ever since we got in the car. It's not like you at all. You sent me a rude little note months ago about my investment portfolio, so I wasn't expecting to hear from you until spring. The Izar Agustin I know would no more take me on a birthday ski weekend than he would fly naked over the moon."

"Am I so unpleasant?" he asked drily. "And here I thought I had convinced you otherwise tonight. At some length."

Her delicate skin flamed red, which only made her look more exquisite and delicate at once, but she still kept her gaze on him, steady and clear.

"I've already slept with you, so this can't

possibly be some ham-fisted attempt at seduction."

Izar was starting to think she had no idea how insulting she was. Because if it was deliberate, it would mean she had the sort of death wish that likely required medical intervention. Meanwhile, he was standing entirely too straight. Like a statue of himself.

"Allow me to assure you that you are the only woman alive who has ever described anything I did, much less my seduction methods, as *hamfisted*," he told her. Stiffly.

"You don't seduce, Izar. You threaten and overwhelm." Liliana shrugged, but the offhandedness of the gesture didn't reach her eyes. "Why waste time on seduction when anything and everything you want is thrown at you? I don't blame you for being more a sledgehammer than a soft touch."

There was not one single part of him that wanted to be anything like a *soft touch* in any respect, and yet he did not particularly care for being called the sledgehammer in this scenario, either. He found his jaw was set.

She was getting to him. Again. It was unacceptable.

"When did you become so unpredictable?" he asked her softly. "I told you I prefer you obedient and docile. The way you have been for years, or, believe me, I would have intervened sooner."

She smiled. It was not a real smile. It was a sophisticated twist of her lips that made her look every bit the Brooks heiress. Powerful and elegant. It seared through him like a bolt of lightning.

"I should have mentioned this before," she said in much the same tone he'd used on her. "That was an act."

"If it was all an act, you would not now spend half your time red in the face when you meet my gaze," he told her, almost offhandedly, as if the notion she might have been playing him while he'd imagined she was a cossetted princess locked away somewhere safe didn't bother him. Intensely. "I would be very careful, little girl, that you do not overplay your hand."

He looked away from his maddening ward when his aide appeared and nodded at him, indicating the man had done as asked and had located her passport. He inclined his head, giving permission for takeoff, and went to take his own seat.

"I'm not playing a game," she said after a moment, and he noticed with a certain satisfaction that she was looking at the floor, not at him. "I only want to understand." She waved her hand in the space between them. "You've avoided me for a decade. It seems unlike you to suddenly want *more* time with me."

"I told you there would be consequences to what happened tonight. Did you imagine I said that to be droll?"

He'd said it to himself, he was aware. But he didn't tell her that.

"I have never imagined you to be anything remotely like droll." Her blue eyes met his. "But this is all beginning to sound like a threat."

He ignored that as the plane started taxiing down the runway, because it was done. He'd made the mistake, yes. But he'd arrived at the solution almost instantly.

"One consequence is this." He smiled at her then, and he was surprised to find that he was enjoying himself far more than perhaps he should. "We are getting married."

# CHAPTER FIVE

LILIANA STARED BACK at him in shock as the powerful jet surged down the runway and leaped into the air, telling herself it was the sudden upward thrust into the night sky that made it hard to breathe for a moment. That was all.

It was certainly not that insane part of her that spun a little madly and hummed a bit too loudly at the idea of marrying Izar.

*That can't happen*, she told her traitorous body sternly. *That can never, ever happen.*

Because the very idea was laughable. Of course it was. And not only because he was sitting across from her in this gold-plated and overly polished airplane cabin, as remote and forbidding as if he was one of his chilly letters, studying her with a cold ruthlessness she suspected was typical for him. Not exactly how she'd imagined being proposed to someday, if she was entirely honest with herself.

"I can't get married," she told him, once she

could speak past the pressure in her head that had precious little to do with altitude.

"Can you not?" Izar was lounging on the low-slung couch opposite her, his arms spread out along its back as if he made marriage proposals seventeen times a day. It made her feel...edgy. "I believe you need only your guardian's blessing to marry. Between you and me, I suspect he will give it."

Was that an attempt at levity? From Izar—the last person on earth she'd consider likely to make any sort of joke, ever? Liliana sat up straighter in her own seat. She'd never felt like this before in all her life—simultaneously more aware of her body than she'd ever been before and yet as if she'd been flung across the cabin to observe this impossible scene from afar. She hardly knew how to process it. And Izar, meanwhile, merely sat there in that calm, powerfully restrained way of his, as if he was *this close* to exploding—though he never did.

"*We* can't get married," she amended after a moment, when she was certain she could tamp down on the riot inside of her and sound at least a little bit like a rational adult.

"Why not?"

He sounded genuinely curious. Liliana frowned at him. The urge to tuck herself away in her usual, comfortable shell was strong. More than strong—

it was as if her bones want to curl in on themselves, the better to hide her from the searing power of her guardian's dark gaze.

But once again she felt split in two. There was how she'd always behaved, which hadn't ever led anywhere she'd wanted to go. Her strict boarding school, for example. A constrained little life where she was always the outsider. The odd one out. And then there was how she'd behaved around Izar since she'd found him in her bedroom tonight. Maybe it wasn't all wine. Maybe wine was the catalyst and this was the version of herself she'd always wanted to let out. Maybe his presence had simply…opened her up.

And she couldn't bear the thought that they would fall back into their usual roles now. That Izar would retreat into his aloofness and she would cease to exist for him outside of a few scribbled lines here and there. That even now, even after what had happened and the fact he had been *inside* her, he would treat her as if she was nothing more than his ward.

As if she would never be anything but his ward.

There was nothing in his suggestion of marriage that made her imagine any of that would change. And Liliana didn't care particularly to examine all the feelings that swirled around inside her at that thought.

"You don't like me," she said, testing herself. But she didn't cringe away the moment the words left her mouth. She didn't automatically lower her eyes or make her voice soft and apologetic the way no small part of her urged her to do. Her voice was even. "And forgive me, but I'm not all that fond of you."

His hard mouth flirted with the faintest curve, and Liliana felt it the way she had back in her apartment, as if he was licking that fire all over her skin. She had to fight to repress a telling little shiver.

"Perhaps you are too inexperienced to realize that when a woman comes apart in a man's arms as you did tonight, it suggests a certain fondness whether she is cognizant of it or not." He shrugged, as much with his chin as with his shoulder, reminding her how very Spanish he was. "But in any case, this sounds a great deal like every marriage I have ever witnessed."

"Cynicism is not attractive," she dared to tell him. "Surely one of your nine thousand paramours—this year, anyway—must have mentioned this to you at one point or another."

Izar laughed. *Laughed.* She had the vague, muddled impression that he might have laughed while they'd both been stretched out on her bed and the world had gone mad, but this was different. Much different. It wrapped around her even as it cascaded through her. It held her so tight she wasn't sure she'd ever move again. Nor wish to.

"I am not cynical, *gatita*. I am a realist, that is all." The laughter faded from his voice, his simmering black eyes. He looked almost kind then, and that was enough to raise the fine hairs on the back of her neck. "I do not require that you fall in love with me, if that is your concern."

"Did you imagine that was likely?" she managed to say, hoping against hope that he couldn't possibly know how hard her heart kicked at her at that word. *Love.* That dangerous, impossible word that had no place here. It made her dizzy to hear it on his lips.

"Innocent girls are forever imagining themselves in love," Izar replied, condescending and insulting at once. She had the sense it was deliberate—but that hardly made it any better. "This is the danger of deflowering virgins, of course. There are usually emotions. Recriminations. Pleas and promises, et cetera."

Liliana thought her jaw might have turned to metal, it was so tight.

"Let me hasten to assure you that you're perfectly safe from me."

"I am pleased to hear it." He studied her a moment. "Then there should be no silliness or misplaced missishness about marrying me, no?"

*Missish*, Liliana thought, was one of the most patronizing words she'd ever heard in her life. Particularly tonight. She had to ignore it—or give in to her simmering temper and hurl something heavy at him.

She opted for the former. Barely.

"The only silliness is that you would even mention marriage." When he continued to do absolutely nothing but sit there and *watch* her, with that hint of a curve to his mouth and that glitter in his dark gaze as if he knew all kinds of things she did not, Liliana plowed on. "You don't know me. You don't *want* to know me or you might have made an effort to do so at some point in the past decade."

If possible, he looked bored. "Is that necessary? I certainly do not expect you to *know me*. That sounds a ghastly and uncomfortable exercise. I am talking of marriage, Liliana, not an excavation."

She was only aware she'd curled her hands into fists when she felt her nails dig into her palms. But ordering herself to unclench her fingers didn't seem to work, so she ignored the sharp little sting and kept on.

"What do you think a marriage is?" she asked him. Incredulous—and something else. Something that felt a whole lot more like *insulted*, which she was terrified was entirely too close to *hurt*. "Because I think you'll find it's a little more complicated than your usual relationships, which require only that a woman of appropriate looks hangs on your arm, keeps her smile bright and her neckline low, and never, ever questions you. About anything."

Again, that laugh of his, which should not have struck her as so…disastrously marvelous.

"The only thing you know less about than relationships in general is a relationship with me," Izar replied. Did she imagine that his tone was darker? That his gaze was harder? Or was it her body's reaction to him that made it seem that way? "I beg you, do not embarrass yourself, *gatita*."

Liliana was past embarrassment. She was into a whole new realm that was half humiliated and half furious, and she felt like nothing so much as an overinflated balloon stretched thin and on the verge of popping. She focused on him, instead.

"I was only speculating, of course, the way every tabloid in the world does every time you venture into public with the latest model. Though I should tell you, this conversation is not exactly changing my mind."

Izar smiled faintly. "I do not recall asking you a question that required your input."

"I'm not marrying you." She belted that out

and it felt good, no matter how odd and hollow she felt inside. As if she was arguing against herself instead of *for* herself. She had no choice but to take it further, to prove she would never be so masochistic. "I would rather die than marry you and, no, that's not melodrama. That's a fact."

Izar's dark eyes gleamed, but he said nothing as the air steward appeared and fixed him a drink without his needing to order one, offered Liliana only sparkling water, then fussed about with several platters of hors d'oeuvres.

"Did you ask him not to give me a drink?" she asked the moment the man left. "Was there a secret signal?"

"It is standard protocol not to ply impressionable young women with alcoholic beverages unless they request them." Izar's head tilted slightly to one side as he swirled his own drink in its glass, the sharp scent of it crisp in the air between them. "Or do you imagine my staff can discern your wishes from the ether? They are good, of course. But no one is that good, I'm afraid."

Liliana forced herself to stop gritting her teeth. She leaned forward slightly, glaring at him, and it was suddenly unbelievable to her that she'd ever felt intimidated by this man. From across oceans, no less. Or that she'd been entirely tongue-tied during their cumulative fifteen minutes of conversation via telephone over the course of the past ten years. Because her worry tonight was that once she started—and God help her, she'd already started—she'd never, ever stop.

"Tell me what you think marriage looks like," she suggested, her voice a little hard. Perhaps more than a little. "Not in a philosophical sense. This marriage." She indicated the two of them with a sharp flick of her wrist. "What do you think *this* marriage would look like?"

"It would look like this," Izar replied, as if that should have been obvious. He took a pull from his drink and settled back against the sofa again. "Well. Not precisely *this*. I cannot say I find your belligerence attractive."

"That is heartbreaking news," she murmured. "I am devastated to hear it."

Izar's dark gaze slid to hers, as if her sarcasm was a slap. "I am willing to overlook the night's excesses, as it did provide a bit of clarity in the end. But let me be clear. I do not intend to lie in a marital bed built of spite. I do not plan to spend my days fencing words with my wife. That holds no appeal for me at all."

"Then I suggest you find yourself the appropriate automaton and practice your nonproposals on her," Liliana retorted.

Izar sighed slightly, then settled back against the sofa as if he had never been more at his ease in all his charmed life.

"I expect my wife to be beautiful yet modest, and never showy or common," he told her. Very much as if she hadn't spoken. "She must exude elegance at all times, in public and private. No slouching, Liliana, or clothes that would better suit an overwrought American teen in the midst of an identity crisis. No flinging herself on the furniture or stamping her feet, like an obstreperous child. She must always appear sophisticated in public, beyond reproach with exquisite manners, but must never become jaded. She must be as obedient as she is educated. Interesting without ever becoming attention seeking. I have no patience for petty squabbles in public or private, extended interrogations about my decisions or tiresome, manipulative negotiations over sex."

"You are describing an animated corpse, I think. Or a blow-up doll."

"There will certainly be no back talk or smart remarks in my marriage, so I would suggest you get them out now. My wife must be prepared to act as my second when necessary, particularly in business situations, but must never imagine herself my equal."

"Certainly not. The world would crumble beneath our feet were this paragon to make such a crass and overreaching error."

His brows rose at her dry, arch tone, but he didn't address it.

"I will require an heir at some point, of course. Perhaps two children, but no more. They will have to share the running of an empire, after all, and that will be difficult to do if there are too many competing factions."

Liliana felt pale, though there was no reason for it. After all, her guardian's cold-blooded approach to matrimony had nothing to do with her, no matter what he said or seemed to believe. She would watch from afar and pity his eventual wife, but that was as much as it would affect her.

There was absolutely no reason for that hard knot in her stomach, then. None at all.

"I view a marriage as no different from any business arrangement," he was saying in that same arrogant, high-handed way of his, cradling his drink in his large, remarkably clever hand. And she knew exactly how clever now, didn't she? "Though it is in many ways more simple, as its success will not depend on the market."

"Do you lecture your business associates about the dangers of tiresome, manipulative negotiations over sex?" she asked when it seemed he'd run through his awful little list of preferred attributes, like the world's most offensive personal ad. "Because if so, I'm suddenly much more interested in entering the corporate world. I'd always heard it was far more boring."

"When in doubt, Liliana, remember that there is a hierarchy." His black eyes gleamed. "Just as there is now. I make the decisions. You abide by them. Nothing could be simpler."

He lifted his drink to his lips as if the conversation was over. And Liliana found she was no longer anything like furious. She felt...deflated, almost. And so cold inside she worried that if she started to shiver it might tear her apart.

"Izar." She waited for him to look at her. Of course he took his time. "You must know that no woman would ever sign up for that. Any of that. It's insulting at best."

Again, that quirk in the corner of his arrogant mouth that should not have felt wired directly into her core. "You underestimate the draw, I think."

"You have yet to mention any draw at all. It's all medieval rules and what I suspect must be a deep vein of the worst sort of misogyny. Which, in case you wondered, is moving past *unattractive* into the realm of *actively horrifying*. And is not, in any sense of the word, a draw."

"The draw, *gatita*—" and he didn't smile then. He didn't have to smile. But his eyes seemed to glow with a very male knowledge that undid her "—is me."

That sat there between them, humming and spinning over plates of fine cheese and cured meats. And Liliana was appalled to feel something inside her soften, against her own wishes. As if some part of her actually yearned for that cold, austere, robotic life he'd just described— but that was impossible, surely. She would have to hate herself very deeply indeed to choose to erase herself like that in service to a man so stern, so unreachable. Or she would have to be entirely mad.

Unbidden, her mind trotted out one vivid image after the next from earlier in the evening. Taunting her. Shaming her. *Perhaps you are too inexperienced to realize that when a woman comes apart in a man's arms as you did tonight, it suggests a certain fondness,* he'd said. Dreadful man.

Yet there was no denying the fact that she had done exactly that. Again and again. And wanted to again, to her shame. She pulled in a breath.

Liliana had spent too long under his thumb already, and thank God it had only been figurative. She'd had only four short years at Barnard plus the few months since trying to figure out who she was. She couldn't shortchange herself now. She couldn't give up. And certainly not when it was for so little. A man she hardly knew. A man who fascinated her far more than he should, yes, but who couldn't even stir himself to work up a marriage proposal that wasn't as much an insulting slap in the face as it was an invitation.

Liliana had been twelve—not two—when her parents had died. That meant she remembered them. Looking at all the pictures of them in magazines and online, it was tempting to lose herself in her mother's effortless beauty or her father's tawny good looks, but she remembered the other side of all the elegant photographs. They'd laughed. They'd huddled together on the sofa in front of the fire and talked for hours. They'd taken long walks in the country, always holding hands. They'd had tempestuous fights in three languages, and her mother even threw breakable things when it suited her, but they'd always settled their disagreements one way or another before the next morning. They'd prided themselves on that. Sometimes, when she was meant to be in bed, Liliana would catch them dancing in slow sweeps around the front hall and into the various living rooms, their eyes closed and their arms tight around each other.

Her parents had loved each other. She had no doubt. They had loved each other fiercely and passionately, and they had loved her much the same way. More than this, they'd enjoyed each other's company. They'd listened to each other. When they were apart they would call each other, and Liliana could remember the way they'd talked about their separate days as if it was necessary for both of them to know all the details of each. Then they'd whisper things she could only imagine now, things they'd likely not wanted their child to overhear. She could remember her mother's low laugh, her father's deep voice, each spiced with what she could only describe, in retrospect, as endless longing.

Her parents had truly loved each other. Liliana had no intention of settling for anything less than that. It would be a betrayal of them, of the lives they'd led and had lost too soon, of what she imagined they'd have wanted for her.

Some part of her felt almost sad that Izar hadn't seen them in the same way, that he hadn't been as moved by them as she was or inspired to find his own piece of what they'd had—but then, he had been their business partner. She had no real idea what his relationship to them had been. Liliana was their daughter. Their legacy. She could do no less than honor them.

"Thank you," she said politely. After a very long moment. After deciding that it wasn't worth mentioning *true love* to Izar Agustin, who would likely curl his lip at it the way he had at her apartment. And no matter how the word had sounded in his mouth. "But I think I'll pass."

Izar did not mention marriage again. Not once throughout the rest of the flight across the dark Atlantic and on into a crisp new dawn over Europe. Not on the brief helicopter ride from the airfield high in the Alps, dodging between towering mountains and far above the crystal-clear lake that stretched across the valley floor. Yet Liliana felt it was looming there between them, clutching at her, casting an ominous shadow over the spectacular scenery arrayed outside her window as they traveled halfway up a gleaming, snow-covered mountain to Izar's villa.

Saint Moritz itself was as tony as it was picturesque, just as Liliana recalled the collection of aristocratic little towns from the few trips she'd taken here as a schoolgirl, ostensibly to expose the students to the sorts of lives their wealthy, often titled parents and guardians expected them to live after graduation. Plump and manicured villages nestled beneath towering mountains and lakes so blue they rivaled the sky, yet bristled with high-end shops and a particularly exclusive, extraordinarily blue-blooded resort culture in alpine air so fresh and dry it was known the world over as the Saint Moritz *champagne climate.* The hotels were among the finest and most expensive in the world, catering to royals and oligarchs alike and fazed by neither. It was a place of quiet, in-depth exultation in the generations of wealth and privilege that were on display at every turn, some with old-money restraint, others with all the expected heedlessness of the nouveau riche.

Izar's villa was a three-story mountain paradise in the local style, all high wood beams and stout stone fireplaces with modern touches to distinguish it from a hunting lodge off in a far less impressive woods somewhere. High windows overlooked views of the pretty Engadine Valley in all directions, complete with a private chairlift that led away from the side of the villa, up the mountain and directly into the famous Saint Moritz pistes.

He didn't mention marriage as he greeted his staff and waved his aide and his luggage inside. Nor did he bring it up when it was only the two of them again. The great room sprawled across the whole of the main level of the chalet and should have felt expansive and airy—but Liliana felt Izar everywhere, as if he was too large to be contained. There was a fire crackling cheerfully enough in the great stone fireplace and lazy couches strewn about here and there with fresh modern lines, and Liliana wanted nothing more than to stretch out on one of them and sleep until she felt less…heavy. She'd been up all night pretending to be dead asleep on that plane, and not only had that been a bad idea, she likely hadn't fooled her guardian at all. But she didn't dare sit down now, when Izar had turned that intense gaze of his back on her. It would feel too much like surrender.

"I am weary," he told her then, though he didn't look it. He looked the way he always did, in every picture she'd ever seen of him. Perfectly put together in the jacket and trousers he'd been wearing forever. Gorgeous, she couldn't help but notice now. And utterly unaffected by anything that happened to him or around him, as if he was one of the mountains that stood, raw and proud, outside the windows. "I am going to take a long shower to wash the slums of New York off my body and then I am going to rest. I suggest you do the same."

She bared her teeth at him because it was that or weep. "I would sooner chew off my own arm than join you."

"Such drama," he chided her, and she thought for a moment there was something like laughter in his dark gaze. But that couldn't be. Especially not when he tilted his head to one side. "Did I ask you to join me?"

"You asked me to marry you," she pointed

out, through lips that felt thick and stiff. "Who knows what crazy thing might come out of your mouth next?"

"Ah, but I did not ask." He didn't move, and still it seemed as if he grew even bigger. As if he took over the whole of the vast room. As if his hands were wrapped tight around her chest, making it hard to breathe. "I did not fling myself to my knees and tell you grandiose lies about my feelings. I told you what was going to happen next, that is all."

"It will never happen, Izar," she vowed, and she told herself the dark thing in her voice was as much the jet lag as that wave of emotion she would rather pretend wasn't there at all. And certainly had nothing to do with what he'd just said, his words punching through her like bullets and leaving no exit wounds. "Not next. Not ever. I will never marry you."

He shrugged as if it was of no matter to him one way or the other. Or, she realized after a moment, more as if her protestations were pointless.

"If you say so. When you are ready to stop pretending you've been victimized in some terrible way by a luxurious private flight to the known horror of Saint Moritz, the staff will show you to your rooms. If you feel compelled to attempt a breakout, I'd advise against it.

We're halfway up a very steep mountain, in case you didn't notice. There's nowhere to go."

And then, impossibly, he turned and walked away. Casually and without looking back. He left her standing there as if he really did expect her to gather herself together like a sulky child, have a tantrum perhaps, but then obey him.

And why wouldn't he? She'd always obeyed him before. Why should he take her seriously? Tonight was the first time she'd ever directly contradicted a single order he'd given to her, much less outright defied him, as far back as she could remember. Usually he laid down the law and she followed it, the end. No wonder he thought she was having some kind of temporary fit.

A wave of exhaustion swept over her then. Liliana couldn't remember the last time she'd stayed up all night. That wasn't the sort of life she led—she never had. Despite herself, she'd taken Izar's dire warning about scandal and Madame's dark pronouncements about the kind of heiress she could be to heart. And of course, she'd never had a night like the previous one. So…unexpectedly physical. There was a pressure at her temples; her eyes and mouth felt as if they were packed with sand, and she honestly couldn't tell if it was the aftereffects of the wine, the tug of jet lag or, more potent than either, the lingering aftershocks of Izar.

She moved over to one of the brash windows, as arrogant as its owner, which stretched up the length of the wall and showed off the grand sweep of the Engadine Valley in all its glory this bright morning, ringed all around by the brooding mountains washed crisp and white with snow. She'd never wanted to return to the Alps. She'd vowed she was finished with mountains altogether after her years in seclusion in the Chateau—but then, Izar might as well have been one of them. He was as raw, as immovable. As wholly unyielding.

Not for the first time, Liliana missed her mother. That was nothing new, but this time she felt it with an acute sort of sharpness that was a bit like a knife in her heart. She could have used Clothilde's advice, now more than ever. She'd spent more hours than she cared to admit going through every article she could find on the internet about her beautiful, widely admired mother, searching as much for the kindness she remembered in Clothilde's famously green eyes as traces of herself in her stunning mother's face. Her mother had been the toast of Europe. She'd dated movie stars and princes before she'd settled down with Liliana's admittedly dashing father. Liliana imagined that, at the very least, a woman like Clothilde—so utterly French and so obviously worldly—would give good advice on what to do when one had accidentally gone and lost her virginity to the absolute worst possible person alive.

Who was now raving on about a terrible-sounding prison sentence of a marriage as if it was 1882.

But her mother was as lost to her as she had ever been. Liliana was all that was left of her.

*And you are not honoring her memory by sulking about like the child you claim you are not,* she told herself sternly. She did not want to obey Izar, it was true. Not anymore. Not now that he was a real person instead of a series of blunt messages. Not now that real person had touched her the way he had.

She would simply have to channel her own mother as best she could. She was no longer a virgin, an oddball, cut off from the world by the lies she told about her identity and the future she'd always known was waiting for her. She was a woman now, in fact and deed.

It was up to her to prove it. Liliana vowed in that moment that she would.

She found one of the cheery maids and let the woman lead her up to a bedroom she could only hope was far, far away from Izar's—though she couldn't bring herself to ask. And then she drew herself a bath in the impressive tub that stood proudly in an arched window with yet another view over the cheerful little hamlets that dotted the valley and together made up beautiful Saint Moritz, the top of the world.

And if, when she sank down into the warm water and let it embrace her, a tear or two escaped, well. She was alone. No one could see her and judge her. Izar would never know.

She could pretend it was the steam.

Many hours later, Izar stood at the windows in the master suite, gazing out over the mountainside and down toward the sparkle and gleam of the villages in the distance. The moon was high, casting lazy light here and there as it pleased, lighting up the snow and making it glow.

He didn't know what the hell was the matter with him.

Travel never interfered with his sleep. He spent most of his life on planes, moving between the world's capitals to hold meetings all over the planet. He rarely slept more than a handful of hours at a time, so he easily caught up with the time change wherever he happened to find himself. Yet tonight he'd been unable to rest for the first time in as long as he could remember.

He knew why. He knew it was Liliana.

More than that—the fact he'd lost control of himself so completely.

He'd spent a long while in his massive shower, his hands braced on the stone wall while the hot water pounded into him, trying very hard not to think.

Thinking could lead him nowhere good. He had taken her virginity, yes, which was regrettable. Or, more precisely, the act had been anything but regrettable itself, but he had never meant to do such a thing. Still, he'd decided to marry her in the wake of it, and the advantages to that were obvious. He might have exploded out of control in a way he never had before, but the situation was now in hand.

Thinking about it—remembering it—hadn't helped.

He'd tossed and turned when he'd finally tried to sleep. Then he'd given up and had pulled out his laptop, catching up on the work he'd ignored while he'd been traipsing around the outer boroughs of New York City in search of his deceitful ward. When he'd exhausted even that, he'd tried to sleep again, but it had been no use.

First he'd lost control, however briefly. Now he had insomnia.

What was wrong with him that he had the very distinct urge to take these frustrations out on her lovely, sleek body?

Disgusted with himself, he turned from the window and stalked through the house, finding his way down to the pool room. He kicked off the loose black trousers he wore and dove into the crisp, cool water, pouring all of this...*rawness* into his strokes. He didn't pause to look up at the glass ceiling and the night sky above him. He didn't bother, when all he could see was Liliana. When all he could feel was her soft, lush body gripping him. When he was damned straight through and he knew it.

This was not what her parents had imagined when they'd trusted him with her. It was not what he'd intended, in all these years of entrusting her to those who could care for her far better than he could. He knew that as well as he knew his own name.

Izar swam until his arms ached and his legs were heavy, but all it did was make him tired. It didn't excise Liliana from his head.

"This is unacceptable," he growled into the quiet of the pool room all around him, in Spanish, and then he cursed long and low and fluently in his native tongue. He switched over to English for a harsher sound when he'd run out of creative Spanish, and then that, too, was exhausted.

And none of it helped.

He pulled himself out of the water and swiped

a towel from the waiting rack, wrapping it around himself as he walked, hardly seeing the villa around him, all its wood and windows gleaming in the moonlight from the windows.

It would pass, he assured himself. These things always did.

Izar shook his head at that as he climbed the staircase. He was not the Heathcliff type. He did not brood and lurk, he stormed in where he liked. He bought out the competition. He dominated every situation he encountered. He was Izar Agustin. He did not...*yearn*.

Certainly not for an otherwise untried young thing who had been, until earlier tonight, nothing to him but another item to check off on his list of responsibilities.

There was no earthly reason he should have found himself at her bedroom door, just down the hall from his. Much less pushed it open. It fell inward soundlessly, and despite ordering himself to walk away at once, Izar moved inside.

The careless moon poured in through the windows, illuminating the guest suite with its exposed beams up above and the stone fireplace anointed with antlers and brightly colored pieces of art. His gaze ran over the empty seating area before the fire, then on to the sleigh bed on the far wall, its headboard and footboard gracefully curved against the hardwood floors covered in bright, thick rugs.

Izar hardly ever came in this room, and he knew he wouldn't again, because it would be impossible to see that bed without seeing what he saw now: Liliana, stretched out and fast asleep. The moonlight danced over her lithe form as she lay there, the covers kicked aside and her wavy hair a puddle of gold around her. She wore nothing but a pair of panties that barely covered her sweet bottom, and he had to fight himself to keep from reaching out and tracing the plump, delectable curves that poked out from beneath the scant bit of lace.

When had he drawn so near to her bed?

He didn't know, but he didn't step back. He also didn't touch her. He didn't trust himself to stop.

Her back was a symphony of that satin skin he'd explored with his hands, his mouth, but not enough. Not yet. She slept on her belly with her arms thrust up beneath her pillow and one knee cocked. And that was what slammed into Izar, of all things, with the force of a truth too long denied. *The way she slept.* So easily and so deeply in the moonlight while he stood here like the looming, brooding creature he had never been.

*Yearning*, it turned out, after all.

He let out a long breath that was too close to shaky for his peace of mind, and then he reached out and gently eased the covers back over her.

And when he made his way out of her room again, down the hall and back to take his lonely vigil at his own window, it occurred to him that it was high time he stopped lying to himself about what was happening here—and so what that it had come out of nowhere and taken him completely by surprise.

Marrying Liliana Girard Brooks would be good business, yes.

But it was the least of his reasons for wanting to do it.

# CHAPTER SIX

"YOU CAN'T LOCK me away on the top of a mountain forever," Liliana informed Izar some ten days later at one of the meals he insisted they share—breakfast and dinner—every damned day.

It was a snowy, blustery morning on the other side of the massive windows, the wind visibly attacking the trees and the sides of the villa, wreathed in snow as it blew itself mad. The press and swirl of the storm made her feel claustrophobic as she speared a piece of breakfast sausage with her fork and pretended it was Izar.

Then again, maybe it was Izar who made her feel claustrophobic. She told herself that was what the sensation was—more intense than a mere itch, like a certain *restlessness* was attempting to worm its way out of that molten, knotted place deep in her belly.

"Can I not?" His attention on his tablet, he

was sipping at what he called *café semi largo*, the strong espresso with a bit of milk his staff prepared for him in a small glass instead of a mug in a nod to his native Málaga. Izar read the papers fanatically, she knew now. From five different countries, every morning. "It would appear I have already done so."

"I tell myself that though it feels like an eternity or two, it hasn't been. Not yet." She sighed. Perhaps theatrically, she could admit. "Eventually, even you will grow bored of this."

She heard a smile in his voice, though there was no trace of it on his hard face. "I am known for many things, *gatita*. Giving up before I get exactly what I want is not one of them."

He slid a hot, hard look her way at that, and Liliana felt it everywhere in a slide of red awareness that sizzled all over her skin and then burrowed deep beneath it, pooling around and around that knot in her gut.

She was certain he knew precisely what he did to her.

"You can stop that," she said now, scowling at her plate instead of at him, because it was never safe to scowl at Izar. "I've told you a million times that what happened in my apartment—"

"Yes, yes." He returned his attention to his tablet, though he didn't look quite as bored as he sounded. "I am suitably chastised."

But that was the thing. He never really was.

If Izar cared that she was going slowly insane, trapped in this house with him, he never showed it. Every morning he came to the breakfast table freshly showered after some or other athletic endeavor. Sometimes he swam in the full-size pool that took over its own separate part of the building. Sometimes he lifted astonishingly heavy weights in the adjoining exercise room. Other times he ran on the treadmill, fast and brutal and sleek, reminding her of the way he'd charged across the *fútbol* pitch. Liliana knew his schedule now. She knew how he ordered his mornings. She even knew that he didn't come by his mouthwatering physique naturally, that he had to work at it like a mortal man, and yet somehow that didn't ruin his mystique in the slightest.

She'd decided early on that it would—or something would. That regardless of his ridiculous stance on knowing another person and how unnecessary it was, she would spend however long she had here gathering as much information about him as possible. In the fervent hope that familiarity really did breed contempt. Because it was very unlikely, surely, that she could be so easily cowed by a man once she knew all the strange little details of how he lived.

But if Izar had any habits that would render

him something less than totally intimidating and oddly compelling at once, she had yet to encounter them.

After breakfast he would move into the office suite on the second floor, where he would proceed to run his—*their*—company all day long, sometimes with endless conference calls. She could sit in the open living room below and hear his voice float down from the wooden beams above, as direct and uncompromising in Spanish or French or German as it was in English. He usually disappeared into the master suite before dinner for a while if he didn't get in a second workout, and she had no idea what he did then. He usually reappeared freshly showered, yes, but what else he did in there with his door shut remained a mystery. At night she would lie awake and try to imagine what decidedly human and lowering things he might do. The ruthless Izar Agustin cutting his toenails? The impossible Izar Agustin crashed out on a couch watching reality television with a bag of chips at the ready?

She often made herself giggle but she never, ever, managed to make him *palatable*. Not in her daydreams and certainly not in reality. Izar would still come striding out of his room at the appointed hour, dressed with his usual perfect taste and fairly gleaming with all of that leashed power and fascinating masculinity that made him who he was.

And Liliana knew, now.

How he tasted. What that massive, sleekly muscled body felt like stretched out over hers and sliding so deep inside of her. What it was like to clutch at his broad, hard shoulders and the exquisite joy that was sliding her palms down his marvelous chest.

She knew those memories didn't exactly help.

*Are you sure you haven't actually been abducted by aliens after all?* Kay texted her one afternoon from back in New York City. *Because you never sound as irritated by your "family stuff" as I know I would be...*

Liliana was curled up in one of the big, cozy armchairs with a book and a hot chocolate made by the excellent kitchen staff. It was already gathering dark outside, telling her more eloquently than any calendar could that the end of the year was coming. And for someone who had claimed to be held against her will—imprisoned—she certainly seemed very comfortable. She eyed her hot chocolate a bit sourly.

*That depends on your definition of "aliens,"* she texted back, looking around at the great room she'd already adjusted to—perhaps too easily, now that she thought about it. Maybe that had been Izar's plan all along.

"Alien abduction" was as good an explanation as any other for the Izar Effect.

Izar—or his minions, more accurately—had removed every last thing she'd owned from that apartment. Every stitch of clothing in her closet, every product she'd ever touched in the bathroom or pot she'd used in the kitchen, everything. Her roommates had woken up the following morning to find a stripped bed, an empty closet and nothing in her desk. It was as if she'd never lived there.

Needless to say, her friends had been upset.

Izar, by contrast, had been perfectly calm when she'd burst into his office the day after they'd arrived in Switzerland and had accused him of deliberately trying to scare her friends half to death.

"They thought something terrible happened to me," she'd snapped at him, brandishing her mobile at him as if it was the weapon she'd wished it was. "It can't possibly have been necessary to scrub me out of there as if I never existed."

"There is no scenario in which I am going to view your escape from that hovel as anything but a victory, Liliana," Izar had replied, without bothering to glance up at her from whatever he was studying on his laptop. As if she wasn't even really in the room with him. "You are wasting your breath."

"It was also a waste of time and resources," she'd thrown at him. "Because I'm moving right back in the moment I get back home to New York. You can count on it."

At that, Izar had raised his dark gaze from his laptop and settled it on her.

He hadn't said a word.

She'd told herself she'd felt the bars of this prison of his slide tighter around her, even so.

*But is it really a prison?* she asked herself now, sitting up straighter in her chair and putting her book aside. *If it is, why haven't you tried—even once—to escape? He's locked away in his office. You're lounging around completely unsupervised. You could be down the mountain and on your way back to New York in a few hours. Why aren't you?*

Liliana didn't have an answer for that. Not one that she was willing to entertain, anyway. It was easier to tell herself that she was biding her time here. Looking for her moment.

Just as it was easier to tell her friends that she'd been abducted by aliens—*no really, I'm fine and just navigating some tricky family stuff,* she'd texted as merrily as possible once she'd realized she'd be in Switzerland awhile, because what could they do?—than attempt to explain the reality of Izar. The guardian she'd never known and yet now knew… Biblically. And only the once.

How would *that* conversation go?

For one thing, she would have to come clean about who she was. For another, Izar was nothing short of maddening. He was never kind when he could be blunt, instead. He was merciless in all things. He was the bane of her existence, but he was also the man who had presented her with a set of trunks the morning after they'd arrived in Saint Moritz, stuffed full of what she knew at a glance were clothes from the company's couture houses.

She knew those inspired, eclectic lines. She knew those quietly elegant cuts. The fabrics and the colors. Of course she knew. She was the last Girard.

The lump in her throat hadn't gone away, no matter how many times she swallowed.

"You are your mother's daughter," Izar had told her when she'd only gazed at him, right there in the great foyer, unable to process what he'd done. More, what it meant. Her heart had pounded so hard she thought it might knock her over. "It is time to dress the part."

The first night in Saint Moritz, Izar had sent her back to rooms twice before he'd judged her appropriately dressed and allowed her to take her place at the dinner table—not that she'd had any interest in eating with him after that.

"There aren't actually a great many occasions to dress like this in my life," she'd seethed at him, sitting ramrod straight in her chair, feeling flushed and out of sorts because she wasn't her damned mother. No pretty dress was going to turn her into Clothilde Girard, and it was insulting—and painful—to try. "I'm an intern, not Cinderella."

"You are Liliana Girard Brooks," he'd corrected her softly yet with that iron beneath it, daring her to contradict him. "You were born to wear these clothes."

She'd balled her hands into fists in her lap and glared fiercely at her first course, unable to see it through the haze of her grief and fear and discomfort. And the fury she'd channeled it all into and aimed straight at him.

"I don't belong in these clothes. They don't suit me. I look like a girl at a sad prom in a dress that's much too old for her."

"You sound like a petulant child," Izar had interjected. It had gotten her head up, her gaze on his. He'd sat across from her the way he always did in the formal dining room, there on one end of the highly polished rustic long table. "But if one can look past that unpleasantness and the scowl you are wearing for no apparent reason, you remain a beautiful woman in a dress that fits you perfectly and is itself a minor work of art." He'd raised his dark brows. "Do you wish to be a work of art, Liliana? Or would you prefer to be mediocre?"

She had glared at him because that was easier than exploring all the things that rolled through her then, huge and heavy and dark. History and longing and more grief and *him*, besides, careening around inside of her and making her feel too big for her own skin, much less the beautiful dress she wore.

"If mediocre means unmarried and left to my own devices and *free*," she'd bit out, "I choose that."

He'd only tipped his wineglass at her, as if he'd long since given up attempting to reason with her.

"Think less about your freedom, *gatita*," he'd said softly. "And more about your legacy."

Every night since had been a variation on the same theme. Liliana didn't know how long it took her to understand that while this might be another sort of prison, it was also Izar's personal version of finishing school. He was molding her into the perfect wife. *His* perfect wife. Night after night.

"I'm not your Frankenstein," she'd told him roughly a week into it. He'd spent the whole of their dinner lecturing her on how to talk to the different sort of pompous men she was likely to encounter while out at supposedly social business occasions. She'd scowled at him when he'd gazed back at her in arrogant astonishment. "You can't cut me up into pieces and then sew me back together into some new, improved version of me that does nothing but your bidding."

"Have I cut you into pieces, Liliana?" She hated when his voice went calm like that. As if he was fending off a child's tantrum. "I might expect there to be rather more blood, if so. I was under the impression I was explaining your place in the world."

"Your world, not mine," she'd insisted.

But he'd stopped bothering to reply to her when she made that particular accusation. And she knew why. Because with every day that passed, she betrayed herself. She became more comfortable in the clothes she wore, because he insisted she wear them. Cashmere sweaters and soft trousers when she would have chosen a sweatshirt and jeans. Layering pieces in soft wools or suedes when she would have gravitated toward basic fleece. All of her choices so far beyond anything a college student might have worn that she was forced to stop thinking of herself as one. And soon after, she stopped feeling like an imposter when she stepped into one of the evening dresses that waited for her in her dressing room each night. She started taking a little more care with her hair, rather than simply throwing it back in her usual haphazard twist. She thought a bit harder about her accessories and her shoes. It was if she was starting to see herself as he did.

She was doing his job for him, she often thought with something like despair when she looked at her inarguably elegant reflection in her mirror. She was turning *herself* into his perfect wife.

Yet, somehow, she couldn't seem to stop.

Tonight she wore a piece from one of the current collections, a gown in a shade of violet that swept from a cunning, wide ruffle on one shoulder all the way to the floor, leaving the other shoulder bare. She'd arranged her hair in a complicated chignon made of individually chunky braids swept back and gathered at the nape of her neck, and she'd added a pair of diamond drop earrings that had once belonged to her mother. Then she'd even gone so far as to dab a hint of her favorite perfume at her pulse points.

She hadn't asked herself why she'd taken the trouble. Or maybe it was more accurate to say she'd deliberately avoided asking herself such questions until she was walking down the great stair toward the dining room as the grandfather clock chimed out the time.

Izar stood at the bottom, wearing a dark suit that managed to accentuate his natural athleticism while turning all that brooding ruthlessness into a kind of hard-edged elegance. He looked like the sort of wolfish Prince Charming girls didn't quite dare dream about. He looked like he knew how to use his hands. And he watched her come toward him with an almost arrested look on his hard face, that muscle in his cheek flexing—and his eyes on the high slit of the dress that reached toward her upper thigh.

Liliana wanted to say something—anything—to break this spell that worsened every night and was particularly lethal just then. It was dangerous to stay quiet when he was looking at her like that. It was more than dangerous. She knew she was risking…everything.

But she didn't say a word.

He met her at the bottom of the stair and offered her his arm. So formal and correct, it should have made her laugh. How silly was this? They were staying in the same house. They could as easily eat dinner in sweats for all it would matter. This was nothing more than an extended game of dress up and make-believe—

But she didn't laugh.

A strange sort of exhilaration was coursing

through her, making her feel *alive* in a way she never had when she was back in New York. It had something to do with the man who moved with such brutal precision beside her. It was something in the way the exquisitely made dress swept against her skin as she walked, like a caress. It was something about his arm beneath hers, hard and corded and warm.

When he led her to her seat and helped her into it, Liliana felt fluttery. Light-headed. She told herself she was simply hungry—but then Izar took his seat across from her and she knew better. It was that hungry gleam in his dark, dark eyes. It was the way he studied her as if he knew every single thing she was thinking and feeling, and had every intention of using them against her.

He made no attempt to break the silence between them, and Liliana thought she might explode.

"How did you meet my parents?" she asked him. She hadn't meant to ask that. But it had occurred to her that she didn't know the answer, and surely she should. Oh, she'd read the articles that gushed about their partnership, but articles weren't reality. They were spin. One thing Izar could be depended upon *not* to do was spin. "I realize I have no idea how you came to know them."

She thought he looked surprised, in his ruthlessly capable way. But if he was, he hid it in an instant, his hard face revealing nothing. That was the strangest part of getting to know this man better. The more she spent time with him, the less she could read him.

"Your mother was a *fútbol* fan," he said after a moment. His dark eyes flashed with something very nearly affectionate. "Quite a passionate one, in fact."

The first course came as Liliana digested that. When the staff retreated from the dining room, there were pretty plates of country pâté with a jubilant garnish of chutney and pickle, accompanied by baskets of freshly baked bread. But even though her stomach felt scraped empty, she concentrated on Izar, instead.

"My mother was a fan?" She blinked, trying to reconcile the idea of her mother in *fútbol* regalia—face paints and ribald songs—with her memories and all those photographs of an aristocratic fashion icon, elegant and serene. "Are you sure?"

This time that affectionate look took over the whole of his face. Liliana had never seen an expression like that on him. Not ever, not in the hundreds of photographs she'd pored over. And certainly not since he'd appeared in her bedroom on her birthday. Until this moment she'd have said the man was wholly incapable of it. Something scraped at her deep inside, dark and ugly, making her breath feel shallow.

"Your father preferred a bit of rugby, but your mother was a *fútbol* fanatic," Izar confirmed. Was that a smile that lurked around his mouth then? "Once I retired from the game and started in business, she sought me out. As much because she'd enjoyed watching me play as because she had any particular interest in what I was doing in my post-*fútbol* career. I think it was an excuse." He definitely smiled then, with an ease Liliana had never seen on his face before. She'd have said it was impossible. Something deep inside of her clenched tight. "But once she met me, things changed."

Liliana couldn't breathe. "Are you…are you saying that you and my mother…?"

Izar's gaze met hers then, something like startled. Then he laughed, as much in surprise as amusement.

"Certainly not," he said after a moment. "Your mother was kind to me, yet wanted nothing from me. This, you must understand, was highly unusual."

Liliana sniffed. "Because you are usually knee-deep in clamoring women, all of whom are desperate for a piece of you."

There was something very male in his dark

gaze then. It wound through Liliana, making her feel flushed. Needy. She directed her attention to her untouched plate and hoped he couldn't see that she was flustered.

"You would be surprised," Izar murmured. He clearly knew exactly how flustered she felt. "Sometimes I am doing nothing but minding my own business when women strip down and offer themselves to me. Can you imagine?"

It occurred to her that he was teasing her. That this odd version of Izar who *felt things* and laughed with an ease she could hardly believe she was witnessing was poking at her, nothing more. There was a part of her that had longed for something like this all these lonely years when she'd been lonely and alone, with only the occasional letter to remind her someone out there was invested in whether she lived or died. But she couldn't bear that it happen on the back of that night in her apartment.

*She couldn't bear it.* And she had no idea why.

"But my mother, presumably, was not one of the naked masses," Liliana said, instead, perfectly aware that she sounded dour and even harsh. *Missish* in the extreme.

Izar's gaze turned speculative, but he didn't comment on it.

"We had a long dinner in Berlin." He shrugged.

"We got along well. More than this, we had similar ideas about the future and our businesses. It seemed like fate to merge."

"I would have said the great Izar Agustin believed in himself and his own glory, not fate." Was that bitterness in her tone? Was she actually...*jealous* of a dinner that had occurred when she was a small child? "Or is that more something you say to make others feel badly about themselves and not something you actually believe?"

Izar studied her from across the table for what seemed a very long time, or perhaps it was simply that she felt so...small.

"If you feel badly about yourself, Liliana, I have only one suggestion." He reached for his wine, his gaze never shifting from hers. "Stop."

"Yes, thank you." She felt drawn tight into a mean little ball and she couldn't seem to stop it. Nor do anything to temper her hard tone of voice. As if she wanted to bludgeon him with it. "That's very useful advice. Exactly the sort men like you give with no earthly idea that some people are not born with your particular gifts and privileges."

Izar blinked. Then seemed to turn to stone right there before her eyes.

*You did that*, a voice inside her hissed. *You made him go dark again.*

"Izar——" she began, because she regretted it.

But he cut her off with a look so black it made her toes curl in her fanciful shoes.

"I cannot imagine what goes on in your head," he bit out, his voice like iron. Worse than mere iron. Blacker by far.

He didn't move from his seat. He didn't burst through the bespoke suit he wore or explode into a rage. He didn't reach across the table and choke her. And yet Liliana felt as if he'd crushed her. Set her on fire. Thrown her out the window that loomed behind her though she knew she hadn't moved an inch. All with the searing way he studied her then, fury like a live thing pressed against the bones of his beautifully chiseled face.

"But it is more than a mere insult for the Brooks heiress herself to sit at my table and lecture me about gifts and privileges." Izar laughed, though this time, there was nothing remotely amused in the harsh scrape of sound. "I was born in a jail cell to an unwed mother, Liliana, in a time and place where her unwed status was considered a sin far greater than her petty drug offenses. They told me I was fortunate I wasn't sold on the black market like so many others. Oddly, I did not think I was very lucky at all. My mother got out when I was two and raised me, if that is what such dedicated neglect can be called, in a variety of slums and on the street until she abandoned me altogether. I was four. My uncle reluctantly took me in, this wild homeless savage he was related to by blood and a sister he had long since disavowed, because it was the right thing to do—not because he or his wife wanted anything to do with an unmanageable bastard like me."

"I didn't mean—" she tried.

Izar ignored her. His mouth was grim, his eyes ablaze. "I had a ball. That was it. I kicked it against the walls of the falling-down slum my uncle lived in because I wanted to kick it at his self-righteous head. I kicked it through the streets while I outran the police, the priests, and whoever else chased me. That was all I did. There was no cushion. No way out. Nothing but my feet and my fury and the goddamned ball." He was so still. Too taut. And Liliana couldn't think of any way to stop what she'd started. "I made every last thing I own. I sweated for it. I sacrificed for it, body and soul. And then I blew out my knees and I started all over again. I made myself into the man I am—twice over—and I made the world I live in, too. And then there is you. What have you made? Except more problems for me to solve?"

"Please." Her voice was hoarse, and shame

was a thick pool inside of her, black and sullen. "I'm sorry. I wasn't thinking."

"That," he bit out, "has been apparent for some time."

Liliana cleared her throat. She felt shaken, all the way through, and she took a moment to sip at her wine and calm herself as best she could.

"What happened to your mother?" she asked. She snuck a look at him and instantly regretted the question. "If you don't mind me asking. I only wondered…"

"I have no idea." His voice was cold but lacking the simmering fury of before. Perhaps foolishly, Liliana opted to take that as a good thing. "She could still be alive. Or she could have overdosed somewhere with nothing to identify her. I cannot say I care either way."

For a long time after that, there was nothing but silence. The scrape and mild clatter of silver utensils against fine china. The faint sounds of classical music piped in from one of the speakers. The candles danced in their delicate holders and the wind kissed the windows from time to time, but there was nothing in the dining room except for the genteel chill of an elegant meal gone wrong.

"I'm glad," she dared to say when she thought the quiet might kill her. Actually suffocate her and leave her for dead. "That you and my parents got along so well, I mean. It's nice to think of them having happy dinners in Berlin."

She didn't say *even with you*, the way she might have earlier. She still hadn't processed everything he'd told her about his childhood, or that dark fury she'd seen in him that she suspected might be the truth about Izar Agustin.

He didn't look at her when he finally spoke. "Your parents were good friends, Liliana. Very good friends. I have felt their loss every day since."

There was no reason for that to feel like a slap. She wasn't even sure he'd meant it that way. But Liliana was acutely aware that she was likely exactly as spoiled and self-centered as he'd claimed she was. Because it had never occurred to her that Izar had lost something the day her parents had died. It had never crossed her mind that he'd had an entire relationship with them she knew nothing about. She had certainly never imagined for an instant that they'd been *friends*. That he might have mourned them, too.

She wasn't sure what it said about her that she'd never considered their role in her guardian's life, when they'd clearly thought well enough of him to leave him their daughter, as well as their business, but she doubted it was anything good.

The dinner wore on. One course bled into the next and slowly, Izar seemed, if not to thaw, precisely, to grow less obviously furious. Less deeply black with suppressed rage, in any case. Soon enough he was quizzing her the way he did every night, forever poking and prodding her toward whatever vision he had of her in his head—only tonight, Liliana found the return to form almost a relief.

"I didn't realize you took time out from *fútbol* and world domination to become the world's foremost authority on manners and decorum," she said lightly during the salad course. She smiled at him, and for once it was not entirely feigned. "You are a man of many talents."

"I am trying to ascertain what, if anything, you learned in that boarding school." He sounded like himself again, which was to say, forbidding and disapproving. What was happening to Liliana that she should feel that as a victory? "Thus far it appears I paid exorbitant tuition fees for no good reason at all. I might as well have set you loose on the streets of Europe to fend for yourself for all the good your education did you."

"I managed to get into college," she pointed out. "Possibly because the admissions department thought my grades were more important than my ability to smile mysteriously at old men who try to paw me at fund-raisers."

She expected Izar to deliver one of his cutting remarks. Or perhaps fix her with one of his skin-prickling glares. The usual.

But this was not a usual night. And perhaps she should have recognized that she'd already pushed him too far.

He pushed back from the table and stood in a single movement that managed to be both graceful and shockingly brutal at once, as if all the violence and power he held within him was visible and dancing there in the taut lines of his body. Her heart kicked at her. Hard.

"I understand that you find this absurd," he growled at her, his voice low. "But I am not here to cater to you, Liliana. I am here to turn you into a peerless gem among women, admired by all the world. I want every man to want you and every woman to wish she was you. This will not happen while you are holed up in a desperate apartment in the Bronx drinking beer and pretending you are one of the proletariat."

"I never did anything of the sort!" she protested, unduly stung. She scowled at him. "I don't even like beer, thank you very much."

"You have every advantage it is possible to have in this world, yet you feel victimized by your own good fortune," he said then, and this was worse than before. Far worse. Then he'd been in a temper, wild and rough. Now he was *precise*. Ruthless and unapologetic. "Your own name. You have been blessed in every possible way—your beauty, your fortune, your entire life—"

"My life?" She was reeling from the blow, but she sat even straighter in her seat, her gaze fixed on his. "I was fortunate to be born who I was, I grant you. But I was also orphaned. Then left in the care of a man who had no time for me, hated and sent me off to languish in isolation. Out of sight, out of mind. I'm sorry if you consider that a blessing. I didn't. I don't."

"I know you were orphaned," Izar gritted out. "But there was nothing I could do to ease that blow. No one could. Instead, I sent you somewhere you could spend your days with aristocrats and royals who had been raised as you were while being watched over by highly vetted women of excellent caliber, all of whom were paid exorbitant fees to ensure your health and happiness. Exactly what comfort do you imagine I, a stranger to you, and merely a man myself could possibly have offered you at such a time?"

"I wanted…"

But she didn't dare finish that sentence. She no longer knew how she'd finish it. This was a long-overdue conversation, perhaps, but she wasn't a ward having it with her guardian. Or that wasn't all they were, not anymore.

And she understood, suddenly, that the fact everything had changed was what was burning along beneath every interaction they'd had. It was the elephant looming in the corner of every room in this villa.

It was the one thing neither one of them dared address.

Liliana had no memory of rising to her own feet, but there she was, standing on her side of the table as if they were squared off and ready to fight. She knew she should sit down. She knew she should do something to calm him down or, failing that, to end the conversation altogether. But she couldn't bring herself to do it. It was almost as if she was…strangely exhilarated.

Liliana had never seen Izar like this. She hadn't imagined he could even get like this. His black eyes burned. He was taut and almost vibrating with the temper she could *feel* pouring off him—until she stepped away from the table, making her dress move with her and revealing that long stretch of her leg visible through the high slit.

His black gaze dropped to her leg as if he couldn't quite help himself. And she recognized that look on his arrogant, beautiful face, then. She'd seen it before, across the world in her apartment in the Bronx, moments before he'd taken her to her own bed.

And everything shifted.

The world. Her own temper and that exhilarated, drumming thing that coursed through her. That hard knot so low in her belly and the pressure she didn't like to admit was there around her heart.

Because she might not know a great deal about men. She had only scratched the surface with Izar, for that matter. But everything had changed in her bedroom that night whether they discussed it or not, and she knew—*she knew*—he wanted her.

In that moment, Liliana understood that he wanted to touch her more than he wanted anything else. It was why he'd stood. It was why he was so angry. It was very likely why he was so damned controlling all the time.

She knew this, deep and hard and true, as if she'd known it all along.

Her mind reeled, almost unable to take it in. All the implications. She'd spent so long comparing herself unfavorably to her own mother that she'd never stopped to question the fact that Izar kept telling her she was beautiful. She'd assumed it was more of his same old game, some part of his bid to get the Brooks heiress parading around in company designs while under his influence.

But what if it wasn't that—or not only that?

What if this darkly handsome, impossibly attractive man really did find her as beautiful as he claimed? What if the way he'd touched her back in the Bronx, reverent and hot and greedy, was the truth of what swirled and grew taut between them? What if it wasn't about the fact he was her guardian and she was his ward, that he was Izar Agustin and she was Liliana Girard Brooks—but was as simple as the fact he was a man and she was a woman and when they touched each other, the world ignited?

There was no *what if.* She knew he did, with a deep feminine certainty she'd never felt before in her life.

Everything had changed in her flat that night. It had started when she'd removed her tunic and stood there before him all but naked, and he... had not been unaffected. He had not thrown a quilt over her or ordered her to put her clothes on. He hadn't turned away in disgust or anger. Oh, no.

How had it taken her so long to realize that she'd held the upper hand all along?

"Why the hell are you smiling?" he demanded from across the table. Surly and furious. And still with that molten gleam of pure desire in his black eyes.

"Because," Liliana said. She let her smile deepen, and she held his gaze with hers. "I just realized that you don't have the power here. I do."

# CHAPTER SEVEN

IZAR HAD LET her get under his skin and he couldn't seem to lock himself down again. He couldn't seem to pull himself together.

This night was already in shambles. He never spoke of his childhood. He never, ever told anyone the dire circumstances of his early years. Most assumed his parents had died, not that his father was a mystery and his mother a disaster—and why on earth had he told *Liliana*, of all people?

And having told her, for no good reason, why had he made it worse by allowing her to needle him yet again?

That was all bad enough. He needed to get away from this spell she seemed to cast on him whenever he was in her presence. He needed to calm down and sort himself out—two things he had not needed to do in so long now, Izar was somewhat afraid he'd forgotten how.

He'd had every intention of walking away

from this disastrous dinner and pounding out hard miles on the treadmill or in the pool until he felt like himself again, smooth and calm in in control—but then she'd moved. And Izar had been helpless before that glimpse of her smooth, perfectly formed thigh.

He, Izar Agustin, *helpless*.

And she'd started smiling as if she knew it.

His untried girl. His virgin ward.

She looked at him like the woman he'd glimpsed from time to time—the woman he'd been grooming her to become since they'd arrived in Switzerland. Breathtakingly elegant tonight, in a dress that seemed tailor-made to celebrate her curves and the slim length of those astonishing legs. Her hair was swept back in a classic chignon with a wink toward a more urban style with those chunky, messy braids, and she'd done something with her eyes that made her look as mysterious as she did exquisite.

He had understood she was beautiful. Perhaps he'd always known on some level that she had the genetic material at the ready to claim her mother's title as perhaps the most admired and fashionable woman in all of Europe, and thus the world. But he hadn't realized until tonight that it had already happened. That Liliana might have been hiding her light under a grimy bushel in the Bronx, but when given the right tools, she shone. So bright and hot it was almost painful to look at her directly.

There was no doubt that the crown princess of Agustin Brooks Girard was all grown-up and more than ready to claim her throne.

He should have been thrilled.

But that was not at all the sensation that worked its way through him now. Temper mixed with need, roaring through his veins and making him a man he hardly knew. Hard and hot and about three seconds away from hauling her over the table and working out her power issues with his mouth. His hands.

Perhaps, if she was lucky, his teeth.

"What did you say to me?" he demanded, hardly recognizing his own voice.

She lifted her chin, her gaze a bright and glittering thing as it met his. As it *challenged* him.

"You can't force me to marry you," she told him loftily. He'd never heard that particular note in her voice before. It should not have rolled through him like that, like her delicate hands wrapped tight around his sex. "And you know it. You think you can talk me into it with all these dinners and your endless disapproval. You think I'll obey you simply because I always have before. But the reality is that you are nothing but my guardian." She lifted the shoulder her gown left temptingly bare and then dropped it, and all Izar wanted to do was taste her while she did it, again and again and again. "If you want to be my husband, I'd suggest *you* try impressing *me* for a change."

Which was not, he couldn't help but notice, a straightforward refusal.

But before he could point that out, Liliana threw her linen napkin down on the table with a bit of dramatic flourish, then moved toward the door as if she intended to simply sweep off into the evening without a backward glance.

Izar didn't think. He'd spent ten days thinking, and to what end? It had done nothing but inspire him to tell his sad tale of woe to the last person on earth who needed to hear it. Instead, he moved the way he'd once done out on the pitch, lost in the moment with his eyes on the goal.

He caught her arm before she made it to the arched doorway and he spun her around, bringing her back toward him and then flush against his chest. It felt good. Better than good. She was tall and so beautiful it scraped at him like nails in his flesh sometimes, but she fit in his arms like a dream.

Like a dream he suspected he'd had, and more than once.

"This is exactly what I'm talking about—" she began, her eyes flashing and her tone furious.

But Izar was done talking. All talking had done was make him lose his temper and share things with this woman—*his bloody ward*— that he'd never told another living soul. It was unacceptable.

He hauled her even closer, let loose that snarling, desperate, greedy monster inside him and then took her mouth with his.

It was less a kiss than a claiming.

She tasted better than he remembered, and his memories were as intense as they were vivid. She went to his head, then deep into his sex. She was far superior to any wine he'd ever tasted, even the vintages for which the company was justly famous, hot and sweet and *his*. God help them both, but whatever they threw at each other, whatever they'd said, one touch of his mouth to hers and she was simply and utterly his.

*Mine*, something inside him roared in confirmation. It didn't care what she knew or what she said. It only knew its mate when Izar kissed her, thoroughly and fiercely.

He wanted more.

Liliana moaned against his mouth and he felt that like a wildfire, deep beneath his skin and down into the place he ached for her the most, hard and wild and bordering on desperate. He felt her arms slide around his neck even as he hauled her closer, angling his head to taste more, take more—*more*.

*He needed more.*

He lost his hands in her hair, spearing his fingers into the delicate construction she'd made of braids and clever pieces pulled this way and that, tugging it all down to tumble around them in a fragrant curtain. He feasted on her mouth, those plump lips and that smart tongue, and it still wasn't enough.

It would never be enough.

Izar was too far gone to take that thought as the warning it was. He couldn't bring himself to care. He backed her toward the table she'd just stormed away from, moving her until he could settle her bottom against it.

Only then did he pull his mouth away from hers, taking in the flush on her cheeks and the hectic glitter in her summer-bright gaze.

He thought that would do.

Izar sank to his knees before her, aware on some level that he'd once claimed he'd never do such a thing—but then, this was different. He wasn't planning to propose to her. He planned to eat her whole, like the fairy-tale wolf he had no trouble whatever becoming in her presence.

*Only in her presence*, a small voice whispered.

"Izar..." she whispered. Her voice sounded ravaged. Her chest rose and fell, hard. Her eyes were big and dark with the same need he felt rocketing through him. He smoothed his hands over her hips and felt her tremble at the contact, but she didn't jerk away from him. She didn't look the least bit uncertain.

On the contrary, she looked at him as if there was nothing else in all the world.

"Brace yourself, *gatita*," he warned her, his voice little more than a growl.

She gripped the edge of the table, showing him that obedience that he never liked so much as when he was touching her. He made a low noise of approval. Then he shoved the acres of her dress up and up, exposing her perfect legs to his hungry gaze. Slender. Toned. *Beautiful*, like the rest of her, all that exquisite bone structure and the curves of a goddess.

Her mother had been more elegant and perfectly dressed than beautiful. But Liliana was remarkable. The most extraordinary woman he'd ever beheld.

And, more important, she was entirely his.

When he'd lifted the dress to her hips, he used his shoulders to widen her stance, smiling slightly as she let out a little moan so needy and raw it washed through him as if she'd used her hands against his skin. Then he simply bent his head and fastened his mouth to the sweet core of her, directly on top of yet another lacy little scrap of barely there panties.

Liliana bucked and then cried out, long and low and perfect. Izar applied suction, spanning her hips with his hands and holding her where he wanted her. And then he simply...indulged himself. He played with her for a long while, losing track of the world in the scent of her, her graceful thighs framing his face and his only.

*Only him.* There would not be another, not for her. He was never letting her go.

When he was ready, he simply yanked on the lace panties until they tore with a satisfying little ripping sound. It had an electrifying effect on Liliana. A great tremor worked over her, from her lovely thighs up over her belly, then even farther north. She was breathing loud and harsh. Izar pulled the panties from her body and tucked them in one of his jacket pockets, then hooked his hands around her hips and pulled her where he wanted her.

"Izar..." She sounded strangled. Wild. Wholly unlike herself.

She made his name sound like a song.

"Hush, *gatita*," he murmured, his mouth to her core, every muscle in his body tense with the fury of his need, his desire. "Let us see which one of us has the power, shall we?"

And then he licked his way into the center of her need.

It was better than any dessert he'd ever had. Sweet and hot and *Liliana*. He could feel her hands in his hair, tugging and clenching but not, he understood, because she wanted him to stop. He could feel her clenching all around him; he could hear her sweet moans, and so he toyed with her.

He punished her and he adored her, tasting her and torturing her, making her rock and roll and press herself shamelessly against his mouth. He thought it might have gone on forever. He would have been happy if it had.

And when he was satisfied, when she was making high-pitched noises that made him so hard it very nearly hurt, he sucked the proud little center of her need into his mouth, hard.

Liliana exploded.

She shook for a long, long time. Then she shook some more.

Izar thought she had never been so beautiful as she was then, head thrown back in abandon, naked from the waist down and spread out on his dinner table like his own, personal feast. And she had never been more his.

Entirely, inarguably his. It was high time he stopped easing her into things so gently, he told himself grimly, and got on with the rest of their lives.

He stood then, ignoring the demands of his body as he let her dress fall back into place. This was not about his release. This was about power. She'd said so. He reached out and steadied her when she tried to stand and started instead to slump over against the edge of the table.

As if, he thought with a surge of deeply male satisfaction he made no effort whatever to hide, her legs had gone weak beneath her.

When she could see straight again, enough to focus on him, she frowned.

Of course she frowned.

"I very much enjoyed this conversation about your power over me," he told her lazily, watching her redden at that. A good man might not have enjoyed that. But then, Izar had never wanted to be a good man—only an independently wealthy and infinitely powerful one who could do as he liked despite where he'd come from. And he'd certainly proved he was that, if nothing else. "We must make certain to have it again. When your breathing returns to normal, perhaps."

He walked toward the door, fully aware that if he did not leave her at once he would take her right there over the table. There was part of him—a large, aching part of him—that didn't understand why he refrained.

She was wrecked. She was his. She was looking at him with so much naked longing in her soft blue eyes that it actually made his chest feel tight. Why not prove his point all over again in a manner guaranteed to give him his own joy?

But the part of Izar that had spent so long dominating the corporate world knew better. He'd treated her as if she was soft all this time. Breakable, like something to be collected and kept safe on a shelf rather than any kind of potential partner. Now he knew better. His ward felt the lure of her own power. She wanted a taste, at the very least. And there was nothing more reckless and uncontrollable than an upstart with her first taste of power, no matter what kind.

Perhaps, after tonight, she would reflect on the fact it cut both ways.

"This..." Liliana sounded winded and still half-wild, sprawled there against the table, and Izar didn't work very hard to hide his smile. "This changes nothing. You must know that. I still know the truth about this. Us. *You.*"

"If you say so," he said, then looked back over his shoulder. "It will be a Christmas wedding, *gatita.* A holiday to end all holidays. We will begin planning it tomorrow."

And then he left her there, still panting and flushed and trembling with aftershocks and a whole lot of brand-new information, to think about it.

The next day was bright and clear, and Liliana should have been delighted that after almost two weeks shut up in the villa, Izar had decreed that this was the day they would venture out.

But *delighted* seemed to be beyond her.

She hadn't slept at all. She'd been too wound up to fall asleep, her body buzzing with leftover need and yearning as much as it was racked with shame at her own wantonness.

What could she possibly have been thinking? Why had she let him *do* that?

Liliana had made herself any number of fierce and solemn vows throughout the long night as she tossed and turned and glared out her windows at the moonlight over the snow. That she would walk out of here if she had to do it on snowshoes. That she would stop acquiescing to Izar's every whim, at the very least. That she would absolutely never, ever permit him to touch her again, much less between her legs where she'd stayed molten hot and ready for him all night long.

But come the morning, there she was in the shower at her usual time, then marching down the stairs to breakfast like a good little automaton. It was as if she couldn't stop herself. As if his pull was that strong, even when he wasn't in the room.

She stopped walking when she entered the breakfast room, which sparkled in the abundant morning sunshine and made even dark, forbidding Izar look limned in gold and very nearly approachable. If she was honest with herself, he took her breath away. A hollow little pit yawned open in her belly and she knew perfectly well it had nothing to do with food. It had to do with him. With the way he sat against the light, his features dark and almost indistinct, not that anything could mute the sheer power of him. The thrust of his jaw and the thick fall of his dark hair. The obviously strong, mouthwateringly lean body that was always displayed with that discerning eye of his, the one that knew he looked even better in rich cashmeres and soft trousers that emphasized all those long, hard muscles.

He was like a force of nature in elegant dress, and that same old *humming* inside of her was only getting worse.

"Do you plan to stand there all morning?" he asked pleasantly, without looking up from his tablet. "You should have warned me you had a penchant for performance art. Let me guess.

This is called *My Fast Cannot Be Broken without an Argument*."

The same as any morning, more or less. Because for him, nothing had changed.

Liliana wasn't quite sure why she felt that everything had. That the world was unrecognizable this morning. Or perhaps that was just her. She felt as if he'd upended her and shaken her silly, as if she was nothing but the snow-globe version of herself.

"This has to stop," she told him. She didn't take her place at the table. She folded her arms over her chest and glared at him, despite the number of times he'd told her that particular position made her look common and coarse like a fishwife, whatever *that* was.

"If you are referring to you hectoring me with that unattractive look on your face, I agree," he said smoothly.

"I'm not kidding. I'm tired of you—"

"What?" He set his tablet aside and turned that dark gaze of his to her, pinning her where she stood as if he'd used a set of leg irons. "Bringing you to screaming orgasm at the dinner table? Or telling you a few hard truths you would rather not face? Or was it the one-two punch of both that you find so distasteful in the bright light of day?"

She hadn't expected that. If she'd expected

anything, it was for him to change the subject
or lecture her on appropriate times and places
for such intimate conversations, blah-blah-blah.
Not to…throw down the way he had and then
wait. Watching her. His black eyes glittering in
that way she felt, now, like his hands all over
her body.

Liliana swallowed. Hard. And that gleam in
his knowing gaze made her feel…restless. Outside herself. As securely in his hands as she'd
been last night when he'd gripped her hips and
held her where he wanted her and licked her into
bliss. So much bliss she could still feel it today,
winding through her and infusing that restlessness and making her…yearn.

She had to stop *yearning*.

"I did not scream," she said piously.

And Izar only smiled.

Later, Liliana met him in the villa's soaring front hall as ordered, with exactly as much
grumpiness as before. If not more, since this
was the second time in one day she'd done as
she was told when she was certain she'd meant
to…mount a protest, at the very least. *Something*, anyway, that wasn't her usual form of
abject surrender to his every whim, no matter
what she told herself about claiming her power.

"Dress for après-ski," Izar had ordered her
as they'd walked from the breakfast room ear-

lier. "And remember, if you please, that this is Saint Moritz. It is not some ramshackle Colorado mountain town that caters to bearded, flannel-clad young men who address each other with various diminutives of the word 'brother.'"

"I have no idea what that means," she'd retorted. Through her teeth.

"Think sophisticated, glamorous and chic, *gatita*," Izar had replied with his usual smoothness. "This is not a time to revel in your collegiate conception of fashion."

What had annoyed her most was that she'd wanted—badly—to fit in with her friends when she'd been in college. There was no shame in that, surely. She'd wanted to blend in for once in her life. And yet now she found she agreed with Izar, which galled her.

Deeply.

It turned out that she liked very well made, beautifully cut clothes far, far better than the usual big-chain-store attire she'd lived in back in New York. Less than two weeks in Izar's company and she'd lost her sense of herself entirely.

*Or perhaps, after all this time, you've finally found it,* a contrary voice inside her had suggested. *This is, after all, in your blood.* She'd ignored it.

"If you don't want me to show up in a ratty sweatshirt, Izar, you should say so. It isn't hard.

'Liliana, please don't wear a ratty sweatshirt.' See how easy that was?" She'd scowled at him. "And I'll wear what I like."

But she hadn't slouched down to meet him in anything resembling a sweatshirt and baggy jeans, and not only because he'd provided her with a wardrobe that excluded anything he disliked. Somehow, when she'd gone to defy him while dressing, she'd ended up in thick leggings and a deceptively casual wool dress. She'd draped herself in scarves, shrugged into a cropped puffy jacket and pulled on a pair of snow-ready boots topped with faux fur.

She looked like every picture of every celebrity she'd ever seen grace the streets of Saint Moritz. Liliana told herself she hated herself for it.

*"Estás bella,"* Izar murmured, opening the door for her.

And then she had to lie and tell herself she didn't feel a sweet little glow of pleasure at that. It worked its way through her, warming her from the inside out, simply because he was pleased with her for once.

Luckily, it faded quickly enough when he handed her into the back of a hardy-looking Range Rover that waited for them at the top of a plowed drive that was cleverly hidden from view of the house by a set of convenient fir trees.

"I thought there was no way off this mountain besides a helicopter or skis," Liliana said when they were both settled in their seats and the driver had started down the wintry drive, snow-packed walls looming high on either side. "You *told me* there was no way off this mountain unless I fancied a cold, wet walk."

If she was expecting Izar to look chagrined, she was destined for disappointment. He only raised those dark eyebrows of his, and the fact he wore mirrored sunglasses did nothing to tamp down the power of that steady gaze she could *feel* all over her. Almost as if he was using those hard, capable hands of his.

"I lied," he said succinctly. "But it is of no matter. You have not yet proven yourself to me, have you?"

"I thought I had, actually," she replied, her cheeks flaring red. She kept her gaze steady, as if her life depended on it, because the truth was that she wasn't an untouched virgin any longer. It was high time she stopped acting as if she was. "Wasn't that the entire point of last night?"

His teeth flashed in a sudden, unexpected smile, and another flood of warmth washed over her, this one sharper than the first.

"Not quite, *gatita*," he said softly. "Not quite. But I have no particular interest in taking you prisoner. Prove I can trust you, and you can come and go as you wish."

"How can I possibly prove something like that when you don't want to believe it?" she asked, and it was a struggle suddenly to keep her voice even. "You want to control me, you don't want to trust me."

"If I trusted you, I wouldn't need to control you," he replied easily. Too easily.

"You want me to marry you." She shook her head. "That requires that *I* trust *you*, and I don't. Your motivations aren't exactly clear."

"They could not be more clear." He moved his arm to keep her from jolting forward when the SUV went over a rough patch of road, and then kept it there, and her tragedy was that something in her thrilled to it. The feel of that hard arm brushing over her and caging her against her seat, certainly. But more than that, the evidence he wanted her safe. "I want you to be my wife. How much more transparency do you require? Must I break into song and dance?"

Liliana checked the barrier between the front seat and the back to make sure it was shut tight and the driver couldn't hear them. And she knew she should push Izar's arm off her, because *not* pushing him away was as good as issuing the man an invitation…but she didn't want to.

That was the trouble with all of this. What she wanted was to surrender. To do whatever he wanted her to do if it would lead to him touching her again. If it would make sense of all this time he'd spent hanging over her life. If it would be the answer she'd always been looking for from him, one way or another, across all these years and in between the bold lines of his letters.

What she wanted was for Izar to fall in love with her—

*No.*

She sucked in a breath, stunned at the direction her thoughts had taken. Was she mad? Of course, she didn't want that, not even if Izar was capable of such a thing. She knew full well he was not. But, *of course*, she didn't want to sign herself up for the total obliteration that Izar seemed to think was part and parcel of marriage. That was essentially her own suicide.

And yet.

"I think," she said, her voice sounding odd and hollow to her own ears, though he didn't seem to notice, "that you want me to do your bidding. Just as you outlined on the plane. That's not a marriage."

"You are an expert on the subject of marriage, then? How fascinating, given your lack of anything even resembling a relationship over the past years." Another quirk of his dark brows. "Unless you concealed your veritable parade of men from me the way you did your address?"

"Not at all." Liliana couldn't look at him, and not only because he was saying deliberately provocative, baiting things. She stared out the window, instead, at the half-frozen lake and the brooding mountains all around. "I want what my parents had. Love, affection. A true partnership. I don't see the point of marrying for less."

Izar sighed beside her, and she wished—fervently—that she hadn't said that. It was too revealing. Now he would smash her memories of her parents apart in the same way he wrecked everything else. He would turn her inside out and for what? She couldn't *convince* him of anything. He was like a stone wall, only less yielding.

"What your parents had was very unusual," he said, instead, his voice rough, hinting at memories he didn't share with her. "You cannot sit about in the hope you stumble across something like that, *gatita*. You may wait in vain the whole of your life."

She tipped her chin up, keeping her gaze out the window. "Then I'll wait my whole life. In vain or otherwise."

"Better, I think, to marry for more immediately practical reasons." And then he reached over and took her hand with his, sending a burst of sensation and a bright flare of confusion spiraling through her. Some deep, protective instinct warned her to jerk her hand away while she still could—but she didn't. She couldn't. And his larger, warmer hand enveloped hers and held her there. She could feel the heat of his touch deep in her belly, like a pulse of flame. "Common goals, common interests."

"I think you mean fifty percent of a common company." Her voice was acid. "It's not quite the same."

Izar only smiled, his dark gaze hidden but no less potent, somehow. "I will share with you a harsh reality, *gatita*, but one you must brace yourself for even so."

Liliana blew out a breath. "I can't imagine what you think is harsh. Given what you say to me over the course of a run-of-the-mill breakfast without so much as blinking."

She didn't move her hand from his. There was no pretending otherwise. She didn't even try.

"You are beautiful and you are wealthy," he said in his low, matter-of-fact way. So matter-of-factly that it occurred to her neither was particularly complimentary. They were facts. "If you refuse me, you will spend the rest of your life pursued by men whose ulterior motives will be increasingly opaque. Do they want you because your face or your body is like a collector's item to them? Are they only after your money? Do they have designs on the company? Do they fetishize you because your parents were so famous and died so young?"

She tried to take her hand back, but he didn't release her when she tugged at it. He didn't appear to notice.

"Because no one could possibly want me for me," she said bitterly. "Of course they couldn't. How silly of me to imagine otherwise."

"Perhaps they will," Izar said calmly. "But how will you know?"

She jerked her hand in his again, harder this time, and he let her go. But she could still feel his touch. It was as if he'd branded her. *Damn him*.

"Is this really your sales pitch?" she demanded. She told herself she was angry. Insulted. But she knew better. She knew. Deep down, she kept expecting him to be someone he was not. She kept imagining he might say the things she knew—*she knew*—he would never say. Liliana knew it was truly sad that she even wanted him to say them. More than sad. "Choose you because at least with you, I *know* how little you think of me?"

"No, *gatita*," he said, sounding amused and male and *certain* in that maddening way of his.

"You will marry me because you must. It is the only option before you and, also, it simply makes sense. However scandalized you may act at the idea, you know this. But you will reconcile yourself to it, because I know you better than you know yourself."

She gritted her teeth. "I'm sure you think so. That doesn't make you right, Izar."

"But I am," he said with the easy tone of a man who had not one single shred of doubt. "How else could I make you scream so easily?"

And he even smiled at her as the Range Rover pulled up in front of one of Saint Moritz's grand hotels, as if he knew that deep inside, she melted for him whether she wanted to admit it or not.

*Oh, yes,* Liliana thought as her heart thudded madly and his smile only deepened. *He knows.*

# CHAPTER EIGHT

DECEMBER CAME IN cold and swift.

Snow pummeled the Engadine Valley, delighting the skiers who flocked to the famous pistes from all over the world to celebrate the start of the new season. Saint Moritz, which looked like a Christmas card as a matter of course thanks to its position on a frozen alpine lake and beneath the thrust of gloriously snowcapped mountains, shone particularly brightly at this time of year.

And despite herself, despite all the vows she'd made to stay strong against Izar no matter what he threw at her and no matter how much she wanted to surrender to him, Liliana had somehow let herself slip off into a daydream over the past few weeks.

It was a daydream, not a white flag. That was what she told herself.

"I am astonished that your attitude has changed so much, *gatita*," Izar said one morning as they sat across the breakfast table from each other. "One is tempted to imagine you have suffered a blow to the head."

Liliana clutched her second latte of the day between her palms and smiled serenely out the windows, toward the snow and the sun and the villages clustered at the foot of the mountains.

"I'm practicing gratitude," she told him. Fatuously.

His dark gaze touched hers, burned bright and hot and seared straight through her, then dropped back to his tablet. His mouth twitched, and Liliana bit back an answering smile. It was almost as if there was no animosity between them. If she squinted, she was sure she could see what that would look like.

"As long as you continue to do it so charmingly," he murmured after a moment, "I can only approve."

She told herself she didn't care if he approved or not. That she was doing as *she* pleased, for a change. But the truth was, she liked that he did. And, if she was being entirely honest with herself, she craved his approval more than she wanted to admit.

It was as if, having slipped enough to entertain the wild thought that she wanted Izar to fall in love with her, even in passing, which she didn't—*of course* she didn't, that had been a mad little dip into an alternate reality for a moment—Liliana had decided to simply…see what it might be like.

She'd opted to go along with him, or at least to stop arguing about every little thing. It had been unconscious at first. There was no point discussing who had power and who was in charge, because all that seemed to get her was another sleepless night. Instead, she took pleasure in the way Izar's gaze darkened when he saw her enter a room and his mouth curved ever so slightly, proving that just as she'd discovered in New York, he still wasn't unaffected by her. Quite the contrary.

*I could live on that*, she thought on one excursion.

They were in one of their company shops featuring extremely high-end accessories. He'd stepped out to take a call, and when he came back inside with a rush of cold air from the street his gaze went to Liliana's. Instantly. Hard and hot.

As if there was no one else in the world.

She smiled without knowing she meant to and hoped he didn't see the little shiver that coursed over her, then pooled between her legs.

There was no need to fight so hard, surely, when it was obvious that whatever pronouncements Izar made about stone-cold marriages, there was very little that was actually *stone cold* about him.

Not that she was considering marrying him. Not really.

Liliana knew she was playing a dangerous game. She knew it was something far more than merely silly to even pretend that surrender was a possibility. Izar was the kind of man who would take everything if she was foolish enough to give it to him. But even so, she found that she was helpless to keep herself from relaxing a bit into this make-believe little world Izar had created for them here.

Here, with him—whatever else it was—she could be herself.

Moreover, the high mountains, clear air and dizzying sunshine seemed to underscore the fact that Izar Agustin, her arrogant and terrible guardian, truly did find her beautiful. And even more astonishing, in that warm, black gaze of his that she found she could lose herself in more and more all the time, she believed she really was.

It was as if she'd made a decision, somewhere back in her murky teenage years, that she *couldn't* achieve the sort of elegant confidence her mother had seemed to ooze from every pore, so she'd taken herself out of the running. There was no way she could transform herself from an ugly duckling into the face of an iconic fashion house, so why bother? She'd assumed it was a lost cause and she'd stopped trying.

Izar made her want to try again. More than that—day after charmed and fantastical day, he convinced her that she didn't need to *try*. That all she needed was to accept who she'd been all along, like it or not.

The Brooks heiress. Her mother's daughter. Not a pretender to a crown she'd always assumed could never quite fit her.

Liliana told herself it wasn't forever. This was an interlude, that was all. There wasn't any sense in banging her head repeatedly against the same hard wall when there was nothing to be gained from it. She told herself that Christmas was coming and she might as well enjoy the fact that she was in one of the most beautiful places in the world, high up in the Swiss Alps, where it was all too easy to pretend the rest of the world had never existed in the first place.

And she told herself that Izar was prepared for her to fight him. Maybe he even craved her resistance, her rebellion. So that gave her all the more reason not to give him what he wanted.

She assured herself that this was a *tactic*, a *strategy* on her part, not an actual surrender.

Once Izar started the wedding planning as threatened—which as far as Liliana could tell involved making sweeping announcements, having courtiers fly in from Paris to take her measurements for a rush dress with very little input from her, and then calling up the grandest hotel in town to throw money at them until they allowed as how they did, in fact, have a ballroom available after all during the busy holiday rush—she simply gave up arguing with him about it. It wasn't that she wanted this wedding to happen. She didn't, and it wasn't going to take place. But until she could figure out a way to escape Saint Moritz, there was no point getting worked up about it and causing the sort of fights that would leave her screaming and panting on the dining room table.

Because it was clear to her that the more Izar got his hands—and his mouth—on her, the less strongly she felt about leaving him.

And Liliana told herself it was worth being perfectly agreeable, or at least not outwardly hostile, if only for the way it utterly confounded him.

But late at night, tucked away in her wide, warm bed beneath the eaves with only the moon and the stars outside her windows to bear witness, Liliana knew the truth. It was easy to give in. Too easy. It was like sitting down on a sled and letting gravity whisk her down the mountainside with little to no effort on her part.

*You are not going to marry this man no matter what he seems to assume,* she told herself sternly every day, and a hundred times more every night. *This is like working undercover, that's all.*

But "undercover" with Izar meant they went out in public. Together. In one of the most celebrity-dense places in the world, especially now that the season had started and the holidays were coming. Which meant there was nowhere to hide from the paparazzi Liliana had been avoiding the whole of her life. Especially since Izar wasn't trying to hide anything in the first place.

"We can't go there for lunch," Liliana said one afternoon five days before Christmas, balking at the restaurant Izar named. They stood in the upscale pedestrianized part of the village, seasonal lights winking at them from all corners though it was not yet dark. "There are too many photographers."

"Why should it matter if there are a thousand?"

Liliana hadn't much liked his careless tone. "We have to be careful, Izar."

"I am marrying you in a matter of days." It was not her imagination, surely, that there was a dark undercurrent in his voice then. As if he distrusted her sudden about-face yielding as much as he should. "Exactly how careful do you imagine we need to be at this point?"

"There's no need to rub it in people's faces," she argued.

She wished she could take it back, but Izar only stepped closer, forcing her to either dance away from him or tilt her head back to keep her eyes trained on his. She chose the latter—but only because she thought he'd likely just yank her back to him if she tried to step away. And she knew better than to give him a reason to touch her if it could be avoided.

"That's not what I meant," she said crossly, before he could ask her to clarify what she'd said. Because she knew he would as surely as she knew the sun would rise the following morning.

Izar studied her for a moment that seemed to swell up and last the whole of the Christmas season. And then some. Liliana was aware of so many things. The last of the day's light. The bite in the air and the smell of fresh snow on the wind. The crowd all around them, equally divided between skiers in off-the-slope clothes and fashionable tourists with the look of spas and shopping on their minds. She was aware of it all, but then Izar lifted his hand and fit it carefully, so carefully, to her cheek, and it was as if the bustling street where they stood…fell away.

He wore the kind of thin leather glove that only accentuated the heat and strength of his hand. And it would have taken a far stronger person than Liliana had ever been to keep from leaning into his palm. She couldn't help herself.

She was sure she heard his swift intake of breath.

And she felt him everywhere, as if his hands were all over her bare skin, as if his mouth was fastened between her legs again, as if they weren't on a crowded street at all but were somewhere far more private.

What was wrong with her that she wished they were?

"I am delighted to imagine you have become so circumspect at last," he said after a long while, years maybe. His eyes were too dark. His mouth was too close. "But I begin to wonder if you wish to avoid the paparazzi for different reasons altogether."

"What other reason could I have?" Liliana's voice was barely a whisper. She cleared her throat. And his hand was still holding her there, face tipped to his, and she did nothing at all to stop it. To change it or end it. Worse, she didn't even *want* to stop it. "I've grown used to being far outside the spotlight, that's all."

"Prove it," Izar dared her, intense and quiet.

Liliana told herself she was only biding her time until she could walk away from this madness, but the truth was that some part of her... wanted to see what it was like. She'd watched Izar with his various mistresses over the years, like everyone else with an internet connection or who happened to glance at one of those magazines in supermarket checkout lines. She'd seen all the pictures. She might have clicked on more than her fair share.

She couldn't possibly be the only woman in the world who'd wondered what it might be like to be the focus of all his dark, hot attention, the way she was right now. Right this minute. Right here, on this street in a December afternoon that was already gathering dark around its edges in the run-up to the longest night of the year.

She was immune to him, of course. She told herself she was only acting.

But even so, it was breathtaking.

"How would you like me to prove it?" she asked, and she even smiled at him. As sunnily as possible, to cover the desperate clatter of her pulse. "If it involves nudity of any kind, I'll have to ask that we find a place that is not outside, literally knee-deep in the snow. If it involves public displays of affection for the cameras, well. It's not that I'm opposed, but that you made your feelings about such things so clear when I was younger. It will be hard to set all that aside and really commit to the performance."

Izar dropped his hand, and Liliana understood that she would have to spend a long time in her bed tonight examining the fact she felt the loss of his touch like a deep and ravenous grief. A long, long time.

"But if you want me to prove something to you, Izar, then by all means," she said grandly, and she could only hope that he couldn't sense that strange, gripping feeling that knotted deep inside her. "Let's do it."

"No need for fireworks or theatrics, *gatita*." His face was dark and forbidding, as ever, but his black eyes gleamed almost gold. "I need a one-word answer, that is all."

And then he reached into the pocket of his coat and pulled out a rich red box embossed in gold filigree and so instantly recognizable that a passing woman gasped, then murmured something in admiring French to her companions.

But Liliana couldn't look at anything but Izar and the box he held.

Something inside her howled then—insisting she swat that box out of his hand and run, now, while she still could. While there was still a part of her that knew she should. Her heart was a desperate, terrible thud in her chest, making her worry she might lose her footing in the wake of each kick of it against her ribs. The same sort of foreboding that had swept over her outside her own bedroom in the Bronx swamped her again now, except this was worse. Deeper and darker and far more intense.

And she ignored it just the same.

There was nothing but that splash of red against the snow and the hills and the buildings all around them, cradled there in Izar's big, steady hands.

"Look at me," he ordered her softly, a husky sort of steel.

Far off, she heard someone translate that from English to German. There was a whole world out there somewhere, she supposed, and maybe they were all watching this—but for her, there was only that depthless black gaze and that arrogant mouth of his. There was only Izar.

*There has only ever been Izar*, something deep within her acknowledged, like the ringing of a bell.

She thought she said his name, but she made no sound. She thought she shook, but her feet stayed put on the ground, right where she'd left them. She was flying and yet she was tethered to him, to this, to now.

*You always have been*, that same voice told her.

*"Gatita,"* Izar said, in his voice like the dark of night, "will you marry me?"

And Liliana understood that the fact he'd phrased it as a question was a gift. He hadn't simply grunted out an order and shoved a ring on her finger, as he was perfectly capable of doing. He hadn't tossed a box across the table and demanded she wear it.

He'd gotten something in a box in the first place, for that matter. She was foolish enough that the gesture made her heart leap.

There was a Christmas tree in the courtyard of the hotel behind him, bursting with decorations and tall enough to be seen from halfway across the village, and still the only colors she could see were in his gaze and in his hands.

Until he opened the box he held there before her, and light and color seemed to burst forth, blazing bright enough to sear the sky.

The ring looked like a knot, ropes of diamonds wrapped around and around a single center stone, all gleaming so brightly they drowned out the village and Christmas and even the snow. It was unusual. It was beautiful.

Liliana had never wanted to touch a piece of jewelry more. She hadn't known it was possible to *want* so badly.

And she couldn't possibly accept it. If he'd ordered her to take it that would have been one thing, but he'd *asked*. He was *proposing*, not setting out a list of commands. Which meant that she had to refuse him. There was choosing not to put up a fuss and then there was actively deceiving him, and this, right here, was that line. She knew it.

Izar didn't say another word. He didn't have to say a thing.

He waited.

Liliana had the distinct feeling that he would wait forever, and she refused to look closely at the way that notion swelled inside of her, almost crowding out everything else. He didn't look uncomfortable or nervous about her response. He was like the mountains all around him, unyielding and sure, capable of weathering anything. Everything.

Even her.

Maybe especially her.

"Izar."

His name sounded like a prayer, and she hadn't meant to say it.

Izar only inclined his head, all of that gold in his eyes and so much light and hope gleaming in the box he held in his hands. Liliana steeled herself and opened her mouth to end this game, once and for all, right here in the center of the village with all these eyes on them.

But what she said instead was "Yes."

* * *

When they returned to the villa, Izar swept Liliana into his arms the moment she stepped from the Range Rover. The ring he'd put on her hand caught the light, and he didn't have the words to describe what it was like to see it there on her hand, delicate and exquisite just as she was, and now marked as his for all the world to see.

The crowd had applauded them. Liliana had said yes, though her blue eyes were dark, and Izar had slid the ring onto her finger. Such a simple act, exchanging a word and a ring, but he'd felt it shake through him. As if the whole world had changed in that instant.

He'd told himself he was being foolish. That everything he was doing was reasonable and rational. Part of his plan. He'd opted to do something like this in so public an arena only because it would kill two birds with one stone— it would do the work of announcing their engagement, thanks to all the mobile phones and lurking paparazzi, even as it tied Liliana to him more fully.

Because Izar didn't trust her recent acquiescence. It wasn't the woman he knew, so docile and obedient. He didn't know what her game was, but he had no intention of playing it.

He'd expected her to say no. He didn't know why he'd phrased it as a question in the first place. He'd stood there with the ring box in his hand, waiting for her to reject him so he could kiss her boneless, at which point, he had no doubt, she'd do anything he asked.

But, instead, she'd said yes.

So he'd done what any rational, reasonable man would do after making a purely rational business proposal. He'd swept her into a deep, long kiss that could only be described as wildly romantic, something he was certain he would regret when he saw it in the papers.

But he didn't regret it now.

Just as he didn't regret the way she dropped her head to his shoulder as he moved through the villa, moving in and out of the pools of light from the lamps the staff had switched on as the afternoon drifted off into another inky December night.

He didn't ask her another question. He simply carried her up the stairs, down the hall and into his suite at last.

Izar set her down at the side of his wide platform bed, aware that his pulse was a mad kick in his veins. Liliana stood before him, his ring on her finger and that drugging heat in her blue eyes, and it was all he could do not to throw her down and take her in the next instant, like the animal he'd worked so hard to never, ever become.

He concentrated on her, instead.

He didn't trust her. He didn't believe in the sort of marriage she'd outlined to him, filled with all those *feelings*. He didn't want anything but her obedience and control of the company—he'd said so, hadn't he?

But no matter how he chanted those things to himself, all he could think to do was get his hands on her, as if she was his personal benediction. As if simply touching her would save him, when he'd long since given up on the notion that he needed saving.

He stroked his hands through the fall of her hair, golden and thick. He traced her full, tempting lips with his thumb. He skimmed his palms over the sleeves of the fine wool tunic she wore, testing the feel of her limbs beneath. Then he reached down and tugged it up and over her head, so she was standing before him in nothing but leggings and boots.

"Take them off," he told her. He sounded like a stranger. More than that, he sounded desperate.

But she didn't seem to mind. Her lips curved as she toed off each boot, and then she raked the leggings off her long legs, kicking them out of her way.

And then she stood before him wearing nothing at all but his ring.

A meaningless item of jewelry that had no sentimental value whatsoever—or so Izar kept telling himself. But his body wasn't listening. It didn't care what he *thought* about that ring on her finger. It only knew what the ring *meant*.

*Mine.* The word reverberated through him, like a shock wave. He felt it in his throat. His sex. His bones. *She is all mine.*

Izar shrugged out of his clothes, not caring if he tore them in his haste to get them off. When he was finally free of them, he simply reached over and hauled her to him, picking her up and holding her until she wrapped her legs around his waist and settled herself against him.

And then, at last, he lost himself.

Completely.

It was her taste. It was her mouth beneath his again, at last. It was the way she clung to him, pressing her breasts against him and looping her arms around his neck. He slid his hands around her taut, rounded bottom to hold her where he wanted her, and he took her mouth as if he'd never kissed a woman before in his life.

If he had, he could no longer recall it.

There was only this fire, this madness. There was only Liliana.

Izar made no attempt whatsoever to control it.

He angled his head, taking the kiss deeper, plundering her mouth until he felt drunk on it.

Then he moved to the bed and levered them both down.

And everything shifted from hot to *volcanic*. They rolled.

She was beneath him, spread out for him, and he feasted on her. He took her hard little nipples in his mouth. He pressed himself against her softness. She licked her way down his neck and wrapped her hands around his sex, and they both groaned.

Then they rolled again and she was on top, looking dazed and punch-drunk, just as he wanted her. He suspected he looked much then same—a notion that should have alarmed him but didn't. She slid all over him and drove him wild. She bent down and licked at his flat, male nipples, tracing that dangerous tongue of hers all over his pectoral muscles and the hollow between them. Then she found her way back to his mouth.

And he took her then, ferocious and ravenous. He ate at her mouth. He sank his hands into her hair and he held her where he wanted her, and he took and took and took.

It wasn't enough. It could never be enough.

*She is mine.*

He shifted then, hauling her up further against him and then rolling them one last time.

Liliana stretched beneath him, a lovely arch

of her perfect body, and he thought for a moment that he might lose what little control he had. But then she smiled at him, wide and bright and so unlike those practiced, pointed smiles he usually got from her that it made him ache.

Izar felt something in his chest crack wide open.

She put her hands to his face, as if she was learning the contours of his jaw, and he could feel the platinum band of the ring he'd put on her fingers. It was a gentle abrasion against his skin, and Izar thought it might kill him. She might kill him.

He had never wanted this. He had never wanted her. He had never wanted to *feel* another thing as long as he lived.

But Liliana had never seemed to give a damn what he wanted, and now the only thing he wanted in all the world was her.

He held her to him as he rifled in the nearest drawer until he found protection. He handled it in record time and then he kissed her again, smoothing his hands down her body as he lined himself up with her entrance.

He didn't say the things that pressed against the roof of his mouth, demanding escape. They would all sound like vows, like promises a different sort of man might make at a time like this. Izar refused to be that man, at least out loud.

So he told her with his body, instead.

He slid into her, slick and slow, and watched as she threw back her head and moaned, arching into him to take him fully.

And then he was inside her to the hilt. And it was almost too much.

He took it slow. He set a lazy pace, and he set out to drive her wild, so wild she couldn't see anything but him. Ever. He teased her nipples with his mouth until she was writhing beneath him. Then he shifted, thrusting faster as he reached between them to toy with the slick center of her need.

This time, she called out his name when she hurtled over that cliff, and it burst in him like light.

But Izar didn't stop. He kept going until she was meeting his thrusts again, digging in her heels and even sinking her teeth into his neck.

He worshipped her and he taught her. He loved her and he marked her.

She was his. *She was his.*

And this time, when he threw her over the edge and she screamed out her pleasure, he went with her.

It was a very long night.

Izar finally had her in his bed, where she belonged, and he didn't care to examine that assertion. There were too many other things to examine, like every square inch of his ward's beautiful body.

At some point he had food brought to the room. Liliana wrapped herself in a bright red throw from one of his chairs and then they sat in front of the fire and ate a meal he was sure he'd never remember. What he would remember was how he'd pulled her astride him when they were done, urging her onto him and then teaching her how to ride him right there in the armchair.

And he was only getting started.

He lost track of the ways he took her, the ways he explored her, the ways he made up for all this time he'd had her so close and been unable to touch her. He learned her. Every inch, every groan, every sweet sigh. He tasted every part of her body, making sure there wasn't a single part of her he didn't make entirely his own.

And they slept tangled together in his bed, then woke to do it all over again.

When Izar woke after falling into a last dreamless sleep sometime near dawn, Liliana was still in a boneless heap, nestled against him. Another glorious Saint Moritz sunny day streamed in through his windows, igniting her golden hair and making it seem molten as it flowed around them both.

He had never felt the thing that moved in him then. He ran a hand down her side as she snuggled against him and felt…good. Calm. *Right.*

*Content*, he thought, something buoyant inside of him, making his chest feel tight. *This is content.*

It was the maddest thing, but he was fairly certain he was smiling.

Liliana stirred against him. She stretched by pointing her toes and burrowing her face into the crook of his shoulder, and everything was different. There was no separation between them. There was no stiffness of any kind in her lithe body. He would have sworn with everything he was that there was no pretense of any kind.

She tipped up her head to blink drowsily at him, and something clutched at him. Hard.

"Good morning," she said, in a voice so husky from the night they'd shared that he felt himself stir all over again. Her blue eyes sparkled with that mischief that he found addicting. *"Sir."*

Izar discovered he couldn't speak. Not yet. He could only reach over and very carefully, very gently, brush her hair back from her face.

And that, too, felt like a prayer.

Liliana sat up then, in a sudden rush, her

lips parted as if she was about to laugh. Or speak. Or—

But instead she went still. Her face drained of color.

"Are you all right?" he asked, frowning.

She didn't answer him. She clapped a hand over her mouth and then she scrambled from the bed, throwing herself across the room and into the bathroom with such haste she didn't close the door behind her.

Seconds later, Izar heard her retching. He rolled from the bed, a kind of deep, hard chill working from the back of his head down the length of his spine. He followed her into the bathroom, taking in the scene with a glance.

Liliana lifted her head from the toilet as he entered, then sat back, looking confused and weary as she slumped against the nearby wall.

Izar didn't speak. He filled a glass of water at the sink, then wet a hand towel.

He squatted down beside her, ignoring the faint attempt she made to wave him away. He pressed the glass of water into her hands and then he took the washcloth and smoothed it over her forehead, the nape of her neck.

"Try to take a sip," he told her when he was finished with the cloth. "Just a little at a time."

Liliana sighed, a heavy sound. She took a sip, then another. Slowly, she stopped shaking.

"I'm sorry…" She sounded as bewildered as she looked. "I don't…I must have eaten something strange last night."

He looked at her for a long time, counting days in his head. Remembering his utter loss of control in her apartment. Doing the inevitable math as many different ways as he could and coming up with the same result every time. He watched the color come back to her face, the way it would not have done if she were truly ill, and he knew.

"Liliana," he said, and even her name felt different in his mouth now.

Because this changed everything, whether she liked it or not—and he was certain she would not. But it turned out that he did. He more than liked it.

If *like* was the right word to describe that thing that roared inside of him, triumphant enough to take over the whole world.

This only underscored what he'd known for some time. Liliana was entirely, irrevocably, and forever his. It was impossible to consider that as anything but a great victory. He had to work hard not to show it.

Not now. Not yet.

"I do not think you ate something that disagreed with you, *gatita*." Izar smiled as gently as he could. He reached over and tucked a strand of her golden hair behind her ear and willed that roaring thing to settle inside of him. "I think you are carrying my child."

# CHAPTER NINE

LILIANA REFUSED TO believe it. She refused to so much as entertain the possibility because *of course* she couldn't be pregnant. Not at all, and certainly not with Izar's child.

Even after the physician came, summoned in a single terse phone call from Izar. Even after a urine test *and* a blood test, just to make absolutely sure.

"I think that it is time to face reality," Izar said quietly.

He stood in the door to her bedroom, where she'd retreated with the doctor. He was dressed in what passed for his casual clothes, and Liliana had the passing thought that it was unfair that he could look so darkly alluring when he wasn't even trying. She'd pulled on something—anything—to use as armor. Naked and ill on a bathroom floor was no way to have this or any other conversation with a man as overbearing as Izar. She'd been sure she needed all the help she could get.

Because this couldn't be happening. How could this be happening?

Liliana ran her hands over her belly, but it felt the same as it always did. How was it possible that she and Izar had created a whole new person? A new life?

*A whole new family*, a voice inside her whispered, as if this was a good thing.

She couldn't seem to think straight.

"I don't understand how this is possible," she managed to say.

It might have been the first words she'd spoken since the doctor had handed down the unequivocal news. She stayed where she was on the side of her bed, blinking furiously at the fireplace as if she could read her future in the flames, and she tried very hard not to look at Izar at all.

But she'd never been very good at that, in pictures or in person.

In the doorway, where Izar was so still, so watchful—*so dangerous*, something within her whispered, and not in fear—his lips curled in one corner.

"Can you not?" he asked. "Once again, I must question the value of your exorbitantly expensive education."

The worst part was that he sounded so...at his ease. As if he'd transformed somehow into the Izar she'd fantasized he could be if only he were someone else. Unbidden, the previous night flooded back to her. He'd been relaxed then, too. Very nearly lazy, glutted on sensation and need just as she had been. Hour after hour after hour.

The way she'd never dared imagine he could be. A lover, not a guardian.

But the way he was watching her now made her skin prickle. It was far too indulgent. As if this had all worked out the way he'd wanted.

"Is that a joke?" Liliana shoved her hair back from her face, irritated that her hands were still shaking. "This can't happen. I can't be..." She couldn't say it. That would be admitting it and she couldn't bring herself to do that, no matter what that doctor had said. "I'm too young."

Izar crossed his arms over his chest, and Liliana hated herself, because even now in this awful moment where the worst possible thing had gone and happened, she couldn't help herself. She watched the play of his lean muscles beneath the dark black sweater he wore. Her mouth watered and her traitorous body flushed all over in wanton, treacherous readiness.

That had been the problem from the start. And now she had a much, much bigger problem.

Izar didn't smile at that. Not quite. "I think you will find a great number of women have had many children long before the advanced age of twenty-three."

"I can't be pregnant." The word felt awkward on her tongue, like an indictment. And all she wanted to do was throw that blame at him, hard and heavy, and let him carry it. But more than that, she needed to get out of here. Before it was too late. She ignored the part of her that suggested it already was. "I have a whole life I need to live."

"Oh?" He stopped leaning against the door then, and prowled into the room. She didn't want him here, she told herself darkly. Or, to be more accurate, she didn't want him any closer to her because *look what happened*. She touched him and the world as she knew it screeched to a halt. She couldn't be trusted anywhere near him. "And what life is this, exactly?"

Liliana clenched her hands into fists, and the damned ring was there, catching against the skin of her finger and digging into her flesh. She didn't glance down at it, and not only because it was hypnotizing. But because she knew it would be burned into her brain forever. Not just the ring itself, but that look on his face when he'd held it out in front of him. And that hard, almost terrifying flush of emotion she was sure she'd seen move over him when she'd said yes.

But she couldn't think about that now. Her

heart was pounding and she was dizzy and she knew one thing and one thing only: she had to get away. She had to run. Every day she'd spent here with him was a betrayal of herself.

That she was pregnant only proved that.

"Did you plan this?" Her voice was low. Harsh. "Did you do this deliberately?"

He stopped at the foot of the bed and thrust his hands into his pockets, still holding himself with a certain stillness that Liliana didn't like at all. What was he hiding? Why was he holding himself back?

"I was a virgin," she reminded him tersely. "You should have taken care of this. You should have taken care of *me*."

Liliana told herself that if she pretended her voice hadn't cracked on that last word, it hadn't. And though that same, telling muscle jumped in Izar's jaw, he only watched her for another taut moment.

"I did not plan this," he said when she thought her head might explode with waiting. His voice was very precise—and she might have wondered about that if she'd been able to think. He paused. "But I cannot be upset about it, either. I told you what I wanted on the plane."

"Heirs," she bit out. "You wanted two, but no more. And behold, once again, you get what you want. You always get what you want."

That muscle flexed in his jaw again.

"I grant you that this is sooner than planned," he said. She had the dizzying notion that this was Izar being *careful.* "But it makes no difference, surely. The end result remains the same."

Liliana couldn't sit anymore. She threw herself off the bed and onto her feet, rocking with the force of her own momentum. Izar reached out a hand as if to steady her and she flinched away from him, then watched as his black eyes flashed.

She told herself she didn't care.

"I'm not going to marry you." She hadn't said it in what felt like years. And she didn't want to think about how wrong it felt coming out, especially when Izar's gaze was black and unreadable. But she pushed on. "I was never going to marry you."

"You are pregnant," Izar said, continuing in that still, careful, *frozen* way. "I am afraid, *gatita,* that the debate about whether or not you will marry me is over."

"Because you say so." She could hardly hear herself over the pounding of her heart. "But I think there's a great deal left to debate, as a matter of fact."

"You are distraught," Izar said, as if he was unfamiliar with the concept. "I understand."

He ran his hand over his hair, the gesture so

familiar that it took her breath away. Then she remembered. That night in her apartment. When she'd gotten under his skin. But that was what had gotten them into this mess.

"You don't understand," she seethed at him. "You can never understand."

"Liliana."

But she didn't want to hear him say her name, and certainly not in that tone. It reminded her of all those cold, brutal letters. It reminded her of those few phone calls, all directives and commands.

It reminded her that even here and now, when he'd taken her virginity and gotten her pregnant besides, he still thought he was in charge of her.

Something flipped inside of her, like a switch. It was that stark, that complete. And if there was a great hollow mess beneath her sudden resolve, Liliana ignored it.

"You," she said, very distinctly, "can go to hell."

And she punctuated that by wrenching his beautiful ring from her finger and hurling it. Straight at him, in the hope it would hit him in his eye.

But he was Izar Agustin so, instead, he reached out and plucked it from the air, as if they'd choreographed it.

Liliana felt that as yet one more betrayal, deep and terrible.

"If I were you, Liliana," he said, in that dark, stirring voice of his that surged through her like thick electricity, "I would think very carefully about what you do next."

She didn't want to think. She didn't want to stand there any longer. If she didn't escape this place—and him—Liliana had no idea what would happen to her. She *felt* that like hands around her throat, choking the life and air right out of her.

So she didn't bother to argue with him any further. She gave him a wide berth as she skirted the edge of the bed, then walked straight into her dressing room. She half expected him to follow her, but he didn't. Liliana breathed in as deep as she could and then let it out, but her heart didn't slow down at all. She still felt too flushed, half-choked and *desperate*.

As if she was nothing but a sob waiting to happen.

Hardly paying attention to what she was doing, she yanked out a bag from one of the shelves and then threw some clothes into it. A couple of pairs of shoes. The wallet she hadn't touched since she'd left New York—and didn't that say something about her current situation?

She'd let him lock her away in this place. She'd *let* him, and now she was pregnant and lost.

For the first time since she'd stood in the foyer of her parents' house at twelve years old and listened to Izar take over her life, Liliana felt entirely lost at sea. Like it or not, distant for years or in the next room, Izar had been the center of her life for a long time.

Did she even know who she was without this man as her dark, true north?

"Anything else I can buy," she muttered out loud when she found she'd gone still. She shrugged into one of her jackets, threw a scarf around her neck and then stamped her feet into a pair of lace-up boots with a thicker tread.

When she shoved her way back out into the bedroom, Izar was still there. He was leaning back against the curved foot of the bed, his legs crossed at the ankles and his gaze dark and furious on hers the moment she emerged from the dressing room.

"Let me guess," he said, and his voice was rougher than she'd ever heard it before. If it made something inside her ache, she ignored it. "This is the part where you remind me that you are my ward and attempt to run away."

"I am your ward." She adjusted the strap of the bag she carried, moving it higher on her shoulder. "And I'm not running. I'm going to walk out of this villa. Then, if necessary, I will also walk down the damned mountain."

"And the child?" He sounded…polite, she realized in some confusion. Almost as if he really didn't care either way. How could she be so furious with him and still feel hurt by him? "My child, to be more accurate?"

Liliana waved a hand in the air as if any part of this would ever be breezy. "I don't need your money. You can pretend it never happened. Or I can send you pictures while you carry on wading about hip-deep in pools of Eastern European models, whichever works."

It wasn't wise to think about Izar and any models, Eastern European or otherwise. It made her pulse skyrocket. It made her start conjuring up all sorts of images from last night that she didn't want to deal with just then, especially not when she imagined him doing all those things with someone else.

It made her feel something more than simply sick.

*Just get out of here*, she ordered herself, and she started for the door.

"'Whichever works,'" Izar echoed, as if he was sounding out unfamiliar words. As if there was no translation in any of the languages he spoke. "Is that what you just said to me? *Whichever works?*"

Liliana knew she should keep going. She knew she should charge through the door, down the stairs and march all the way down the mountain. That no good could possibly come from this conversation and that she would regret it, utterly, if she turned back around to face him.

She knew it. But she turned around anyway.

"Please, Izar," she said, her voice harsh. "It's not as if you care. Stop pretending otherwise."

And Izar *exploded*.

He surged off the bed and came at her, something black and tortured on his hard face and sheer torment in his black eyes. Liliana didn't realize she'd moved until she found herself with her back against the wall and Izar towering over her.

"I swore to myself that I would never bring a bastard into this world," he bit out at her, his face in hers, though he didn't touch her. Liliana had the strangest notion that he didn't dare. That he was *deliberately* not touching her. "And yet you stand here before me and dare to tell me—with offensive nonchalance—that not only do you plan to make that happen against my will, but you will further render me nothing more than a sperm donor like my own father. This is what you think of me."

Something dark and ugly twisted inside of Liliana then, but she couldn't give in to it. She didn't dare so much as acknowledge it. Because she had the sinking sensation that if she did, it would swallow her whole.

"This has nothing to do with you!" she threw at him. "This is about me, for a change—"

"We are discussing a child." He cut her off, and Liliana understood that there was something wrong with her that she found the sight of him losing his usual control almost…exhilarating. Even now. "My child, as well as yours. This is not about your identity crisis."

Whatever hold Liliana thought she had on herself, she lost it then. Perhaps she lost her mind right along with it. She surged up on her toes, put her face as close to his as she dared and then made it worse by thumping her hand against his hard, unyielding chest.

He looked astonished. And lethal.

"Have you ever not gotten your way?" she demanded. "Or would the world collapse all around you at the very idea that someone might go against your wishes?"

His eyes were so black they burned.

"I get my way because I earn it," he bit out.

"Is that what you call it? You didn't earn *me*, Izar." She only realized her voice was too loud and much too rough when she felt her throat ache, but she was too far gone to care. "You kidnapped me and hauled me here and had every intention of keeping me locked up until you forced me into a wedding I never wanted. That isn't *earning* anything."

"I must have exerted a tremendous amount of force to accomplish all that." Izar didn't give an inch. If anything, his chest got harder beneath her hand. "When, precisely, did I bind and gag you and throw you in the cargo hold of my airplane? When did I lock you in this house?" He shook his head, his black gaze boring into hers. "You never so much as tried the front door. You could have left at any time. But you didn't."

That seemed to roar through her, simple and terrible. He was right. She hadn't done a single thing to leave here. She hadn't even known there was a plowed driveway because she hadn't looked. But she couldn't think about that now.

"I didn't want to come here."

She was still holding her palm there against his chest. She couldn't seem to drop it.

"And yet here you are," Izar retorted, his voice a low growl.

"I don't want to marry you." Liliana knew that was true, if nothing else. So why was it so hard to say?

"And yet the wedding is in a few days." His gaze was terrible on hers, his mouth grim, and it made her feel torn apart. Shredded into pieces. "You have the dress. You have a ring."

She shook her head, and though she ordered herself to pull her hand away from his granite chest, she didn't. "You forced the issue. I didn't want the dress—"

"That is why you stood for the fittings so quietly, I imagine."

"I certainly didn't want any ring—"

"Of course not. That is why, when I asked you to marry me, you laughed in my face and slapped the ring out of my hand. You did this, did you not? I find it so hard to think back that far. Less than twenty-four hours ago, in fact."

"And most of all," Liliana bit out, aware on some level that she was shaking deep inside though she couldn't seem to do a thing to stop it, "I don't want your baby!"

That seemed to fill the room. It was angry and awful. She wouldn't have been at all surprised if it had shattered the windows, but somehow, they stood intact. Finally, Liliana dropped her hand back down to her side.

And that was when she realized that while the windows hadn't shattered, Izar had.

She had never seen that look on his face before. Tormented. Ripped apart. *Ruined.* She couldn't bear it.

It had never occurred to her that Izar could be hurt. That anyone could hurt him, much less her.

Liliana would have done anything to take back her words. Anything at all.

And that was when she understood what was happening. She was scared. So scared. Panicked beyond measure. Her whole life had been defined by the family she'd lost—how could she possibly think about creating a new one of her own?

Especially with a man who could never, ever love her. Even if he were capable of loving another person, he wouldn't love her. She was his ward, that was all.

That unwieldy truth slammed into her, making her weave slightly on her feet and feel almost as ill as she had this morning. She shoved her back harder into the wall behind her and she made herself breathe through it.

And, finally, Liliana was brutally honest with herself.

She loved him. Of course she loved him. Why else would she have simply...*pretended* all this time? Who had she been trying to fool? Had she honestly believed that she could play along with him without risking her heart?

Why else would she have given the man her innocence in the first place after holding on to it for so long?

Liliana thought back, and she couldn't think of a single moment in her life after the age of twelve that hadn't had Izar all over it. Had she ever *not* been consumed with her remote, impossible guardian? She'd spent all these years either trying to be good enough to please him or telling herself she didn't care what he thought about her each time she received another terse letter—but she'd never so much as thought of another man. At all.

Of course she was in love with him. And of course it was stormy and difficult and twisted inside out, because wasn't that who they were?

"Izar..." she began, her voice faltering. "You should know—"

But he had moved back several steps and was running his hands over his face. She'd never seen him do such a thing before. Such a human gesture—so unlike him. When he dropped his hands away, she hardly recognized him.

"Your parents were more than my partners and they were more than friends," he said, and his voice was so low it made her tremble. Then his gaze met hers, tormented and bleak, and Liliana thought it might tear her wide open. Maybe it already had. "They were my family."

"Izar," she tried again, but if he heard her, he gave no sign.

"I was little better than a street kid, but *fútbol* gave me money. More money than I knew what to do with." He shook his head. "I was feral. Your mother took me under her wing. She taught me sophistication and class. She gave me the education I had never received. But your father, Liliana." His dark eyes were a storm. "Your father taught me how to be a man."

Liliana heard a low, pained noise. She hugged herself when she realized she'd made it.

"I never had a father," he gritted out. "And I lost my mother when I was too young to know any different." He shook his head as if to clear it. "You were not the only person who lost everything when that plane went down ten years ago."

"You don't have to tell me any of this," she whispered. "I—"

But he didn't let her finish.

"And then, worse than the fact they had died in the first place, they left me you." The words were little more than a rough scrape of sound, but they burned down deep into Liliana. They left deep, jagged scars as they landed. "How could I possibly be any kind of father figure to anyone? The very idea was insane. But how could I let down the only two people who had ever cared for me without expecting anything in return?" He let out a short, hard sound that was not any kind of laugh at all. "I could not. So instead, I resented a bereaved twelve-year-old girl. And I despised myself for it."

"Izar, stop." She lifted a hand as if she might reach out and touch him, but the harsh look on his face stopped her.

"I do not deserve a family," he told her with absolute sincerity, breaking her heart in two. "I do not know why I imagined otherwise. I was ruined from the start, meant for jail cells and lost neighborhoods filled with horror and pain." He shook his head. "But you are still my ward, Liliana. It is my duty to care for your needs even if—especially if—they are different from my wishes." He studied her face with those black, broken eyes and she thought he might as well have reached inside her chest and torn out her heart. "I will support whatever decision you make about the child."

He nodded to her then, in some painful parody of gentility when everything was broken and shattered all around them, and then he started for the door.

"Izar." Liliana couldn't help herself. She couldn't let him leave like this. She knew that with every fiber in her being that she couldn't let him walk out the door. "I love you."

And he laughed.

It was a harsh, terrible laugh, but it was laughter all the same, and he didn't seem to care that it wrecked whatever was left of them as it tore through the room.

"No," Izar told her, the look he threw her as hard as if she was a stranger. It punched another great hole straight through her. "You do not. You pity me. And I may be a ruined creature, suitable only for the dire places I came from and the desolate things I know, but I am still a man, Liliana. I might want you. But I will not take your pity as a substitute."

Then, without ever looking back, he walked from the room, quiet and sure, and left her standing there.

# CHAPTER TEN

LILIANA DIDN'T KNOW how long she stood there, rooted to the floor where he'd left her. It could have been a few minutes. It felt like whole years. A lifetime or two and she was left frozen, unable to make sense of anything that had just happened.

She stood in the center of her bedroom while her hands crept over her belly to cradle it, and she waited to see if she would thaw. But she was skeptical.

When there was a noise at the door she looked up, but it was only three members of Izar's staff. They smiled politely the way they always did, and Liliana drifted off as if she was no longer tethered to this. To what had happened here. To what she'd done by being exactly as thoughtless as he'd always accused her of being.

She watched as they took the bag she'd dropped near the wall and unpacked it, and then she went into the dressing room and packed it all over again, but with less insane selections. She said nothing when the maid took her arm and led her down the stairs, and still nothing when the driver bundled her into the Range Rover that waited for her outside.

It was not until the car pulled up in front of one of Saint Moritz's most famous and storied hotels that she blinked and took stock of her surroundings.

"I'm sorry," she said in a panic when the driver came to her door. "I don't want to be here. I need to go back. Izar—"

"Mr. Agustin has checked you into the hotel," the driver said apologetically yet firmly. "Once you have chosen a final destination, your things will be forwarded to you."

And Liliana...deflated.

She let the driver help her from the car. She went through all the necessary motions to get into the room Izar had booked for her. The suite was a sprawling affair with several rooms and a stunning view over the whole of the Engadine Valley, but it might as well have been a brick wall for all she cared. When the porter closed the door behind him, Liliana sank down on the nearest sofa.

And she stayed there.

One day passed, then another. She ordered room service because she had to eat, then wondered why she bothered when it tasted like sawdust in her mouth. She was sick every morning, like clockwork, only without Izar there to press a damp cloth to her nape and hand her a drink of water.

She supposed she slept, but what was the difference? It was as if she was suffocating in gray.

Liliana recognized the feeling. She'd spent years like this when she was a girl. It was grief, suffocating and brutal.

Izar was the only link to her family she had left. And he was so much more than a *link*. He was the love of her life. He was her baby's father.

He *was* her family.

And he didn't want her.

Liliana had always known that she didn't fit in anywhere, that no matter how hard she tried she couldn't quite make it work. She was too strange. Too different. Too marked, maybe, by what she'd suffered and who she was. But she'd always had Izar. She'd had his letters. They'd followed her everywhere. She'd had the shadow of him over everything. How had she missed the fact that she'd relied on him to always be there for her in his brutal way?

But now she'd lost him, too.

She'd lost everything. Again.

It was Christmas Eve when her phone buzzed

and she lunged for it, sure it was Izar at last—but it was only a text.

And, of course, she could no more imagine Izar Agustin *texting* than she could imagine him stripping naked and parading through the streets of Saint Moritz, but still. She swiped it open as if there really was a chance that it might be him, after all.

But instead of Izar, it was Kay.

You didn't mention that while you were whisked off to that alien ship that they'd changed your identity...her old roommate wrote.

Liliana clicked on the link Kay had sent, and then froze, crouched there on the edge of the same couch where she'd more or less taken up residence these past few days.

The link took her to a tabloid web magazine, and she was the headline.

Well. She and Izar were.

Agustin's Latest Goal Is the Reclusive Brooks Heiress! the headline shrieked. Izar Pops the Question—And Who Cares about the Scandal?

But if it was a scandal, Liliana couldn't bring herself to care about it as perhaps she should have. He was her guardian. She was his ward. The article was as speculative and revolting as expected, with a great many insulting asides, but that wasn't what caught Liliana's eye.

It was the pictures.

She could remember every second of that proposal. The way he'd stood so proud and calm before her. As if he could have stood there for the rest of their lives. She clenched her fist and her left hand felt empty without the ring he'd put there.

But the pictures showed her far more than her memories. Far more than the kiss that had taken her over and turned her inside out. They showed her Izar's face as he gazed down at her. His beautiful, arrogant face, not the way she remembered it—all clouded with her own worries and emotions—but without any embellishment. More than that, it showed the way he was looking at her.

Like a man so deeply in love he didn't know what to do about it.

He had asked her to marry him and then he'd swept her off into his bedroom, and it had never occurred to her to question any of it. To wonder why a man who claimed he was nothing but rational would behave like a besotted lovebird. And she'd been too thrown by her pregnancy to recognize what she could see so clearly in all the pictures she clicked through, quicker and quicker, seeing the same hard and marvelous stamped on each and every one.

It wasn't that Izar didn't want her. Of course

he did. It was written all over him. It was obvious.

Maybe, she thought then, it was that a man who thought he was ruined didn't know *how*.

Someday I'll come back to New York and we'll have a really long talk about all kinds of things, including aliens, she texted Kay. Then she smiled, for the first time since she'd woken up in Izar's bed. For the first time since she'd found out she was having his baby and had spiraled off into her own gripping fear. And have a Merry Christmas.

And then Liliana Girard Brooks, her mother's daughter and a peerless gem of a woman if she said so herself, got up from the clutch of that couch—and all that suffocating gray—and went at last to claim the man she loved.

The staff had put up a damned Christmas tree and Izar hadn't ordered it stripped, chopped and burned.

If that wasn't proof that he was a lost cause, Izar didn't know what was. He sat before the garish thing in the private library on the second floor of the villa, staring at the obnoxiously cheerful lights and wondering what the hell he was still doing here.

There was trouble brewing in Paris, at the headquarters of Agustin Brooks Girard, in the wake of those tabloid photos. Ordinarily he would have raced back to handle it, but he hadn't. His phone had been lighting up all day with emails and calls, and he'd ignored them all. He didn't plan to discuss his relationship with Liliana with anyone. And certainly not with a group of overstuffed, pompous businessmen like his board members.

It had crossed his mind that he could lose the company over this. They could push that moral clause, he supposed, if they truly wished it—and after all this time and everything he'd put into Agustin Brooks Girard, he found he didn't have it in him to care. Not anymore.

It was only a company. He could build another one if he wanted. Companies were replaceable.

He heard a footfall at the door behind him, but he didn't turn.

"I do not wish to be disturbed," he said in a voice too low to be strictly polite, assuming it was some or other member of his staff.

"That's too bad," came the last voice he thought he'd hear again. Especially not here.

He turned slowly, expecting to see nothing but the door to the hall. But he wasn't having an auditory hallucination.

Liliana stood in the doorway, even more beautiful than he'd remembered her. So breathtaking he stopped wondering just how he'd lost himself so completely that night in New York City. Tonight her cheeks were flushed and her eyes were bright—and none of that mattered. He couldn't have her.

How had he ever thought otherwise?

"I'm sorry to interrupt all of this very productive self-pity." Clad in a simple sheath dress that proclaimed her pedigree with every elegant line, Liliana leaned one hip against the door. She looked defiant. She looked edible. "It looks like so much fun."

He shook his head and turned his attention back to the tree, as if all those gleaming white lights could save him from the things he wanted to do to this woman. Or save her from him, anyway.

"I set you free, Liliana. You should not be here."

"You are the most stubborn, infuriating man I've ever met in my life," she said with a sigh, and it took him a stunned moment to realize that she didn't sound angry. In fact, if he wasn't mistaken, that undercurrent in her voice sounded like...laughter? "Has it ever occurred to you that I don't *want* to go anywhere? When I told you I loved you, Izar, I meant it."

"Impossible," he grated out.

But his hands had clenched into fists without

his permission and, somehow, he was standing. Facing her. When it was the last thing he should be doing. Not on a quiet night in a closed room when he wasn't sure he could bear to keep his hands to himself.

"I'm going to be the mother of your child."

Liliana shook her head at him, sending her thick golden hair slipping this way and that over her shoulders. And Izar knew what it felt like to bury his hands in it. He knew its fragrance. He knew how to sink his fingers in deep to hold her head where he liked it as he thrust deep inside her and made her his.

None of that was productive.

"Thank you." His voice was tense. Hard. Like the rest of him. "I am aware."

"I'd like you to take these next nine months as an opportunity to comprehend the fact that I'm not twelve years old anymore," she suggested. "I know my own mind. We might not agree. But you're no longer *just* my guardian and I'm no longer *just* your ward and you can't make love to me all night long and then lecture me on what I can and cannot feel the next morning. You can't have it both ways."

"I don't want it both ways." He gazed at her, his beautiful Liliana, who finally looked entirely unafraid. Fierce and certain, and he had never wanted her more. He had never wanted anything in his life as much as he wanted her. He understood he never would. And he should have known that was why he could never, ever have her. "I want you to go."

"No, Izar," Liliana said very distinctly. "You don't."

His chest tightened as she walked toward him then, her lips curved in something like a smile, except less sunny and far more dangerous than any he'd seen her wear before. His heart kicked at him. And still she came.

"Perhaps you are too unfamiliar with emotions to understand them when you encounter them," she suggested as she came to a stop a scant inch away from him, and he was dimly aware that she was echoing something he'd said to her a long time ago.

His hands itched to touch her. Her scent teased him. This was pure torture and it would end in nothing. He'd forgotten who he was, but he remembered now. It felt stamped deep into his bones.

"Enough," he managed to say. He sounded furious and he was—but not with her.

Liliana smiled as if she knew it.

"I'll let you in on a little secret." She tipped her head back and reached out to him with a finger. A single finger. And yet when she poked it into his pectoral muscle, he felt it as if she'd wrapped herself around him and taken him deep inside. "You're in love with me, Izar. That's why you felt the need to come over so noble and self-effacing—the very opposite of anything I've ever seen you do."

He felt as if she'd pushed him out the window behind him. "Do not be absurd."

"You love me, Izar," she said gently, and then she made it worse by moving even closer and taking one of his hands in hers.

He didn't know what she meant to do with it—he might have stared down at the place they touched in a kind of horror—but she only moved his hand to her belly and flattened his palm over it. If there was the faintest swell, he couldn't feel it, but he could feel her. Liliana, everywhere. As sweet and pure as the mountain air.

"You love me and you will love this baby," she told him.

He cracked at that. Shattered. As if she'd broken him all over again. But he didn't move his hand. He couldn't.

"You did not want this child a few days ago," he reminded her, his voice a dark and terrible thing. "Now you speak of love?"

"I was scared," she said softly, her blue eyes wide. "Overwhelmed. I'm so used to pitting myself against you, Izar, that it took me a moment or two to realize I'd much rather stop doing that."

"Ah, *gatita*." And his voice was low, broken like the rest of him. "I am no less feral now than I ever was. You have the entire world at your disposal. You could choose anyone. You will."

"But I want you."

He said her name again, but she ignored him.

"Let me be very clear," Liliana told him, still holding his hand against the place where his child already grew, with that same light of mischief in her eyes making her seem to sparkle before him, like the kind of magic he didn't believe in. "I don't want any kind of spiteful marriage. No fighting for supremacy at the table every night. I expect very little, really. I will love you. I think I always have. And all you need to do is love me in return."

"Liliana." But it was hardly a word at all.

"I know you have a great many more requirements," she said softly, "but I don't. I want you. I want this."

"I love you," he said, because he couldn't stop himself. He couldn't keep it inside. It burst out of him, and he didn't know why he'd thought the words were so terrifying and wrong when she smiled at him like that. "I do not care about the rest of it. I have never loved anything in all my life, my *gatita*, but you."

"I know, you silly man," she whispered, her eyes shining and bright. "I know."

And this time when he kissed her, it was forever.

He could taste it. He meant it.

And he might stop being Liliana's guardian the moment he married her—and he had every intention of marrying her—but he would spend the rest of his life protecting her either way.

It was only when she laughed up at him that he realized he'd said all of that out loud, pressing kisses in between his words all over her upturned face.

"I know you will, my love," Liliana told him. "You can start right now."

And so Izar did. Right there before the fire, in the sparkling lights of their very first Christmas tree.

Izar Agustin married his ward on the day after Christmas in one of the most elegant weddings Europe had ever seen, which was saying something. She wore an exquisite dress from one of her own couture houses, was draped in her mother's jewels and featured a veil that had been in her father's family for generations.

"I want them with us," she told him at the reception, where they danced together in a very crowded hall and saw nothing but each other.

"Your parents will always be with us," Izar told her.

He wasn't sure he believed it. But he wanted to believe it, and he thought that counted for something.

They weathered the storm their relationship caused by ignoring it. If the board had issues with Izar marrying Liliana, they certainly didn't mention it to either one of their faces when Liliana took her place in the company.

And once she started to show, no one mentioned it at all.

"It is amazing, *gatita*, how much the world wants a happy ending," he told his wife one night in their Parisian home. She was huge with his child and, if anything, it had made her more beautiful. She had her feet in his lap and her head tipped back over the side of the sofa, but she lifted it to study him for a moment.

"The world may want it," she agreed. "But you deserve it, Izar. I promise you."

He wanted to believe it. Oh, how he wanted to believe it.

Their daughter was born in Paris a few weeks later, delivered into his very own hands, red faced and vocal. Two years later she was followed by a son, chubby and mad.

Izar had never believed in love. Not for him. But he would accept nothing less for his children and the woman who had given them to him. And slowly he began to believe in it for himself, too. Slowly and surely, one year into the next, until it was hard to remember he'd ever considered himself ruined.

One afternoon while the children were in school, Izar stopped outside the gleaming office adjoining his that Liliana had claimed years back. She sat at the round table she used for meetings, poring over sketches, and for some reason he remembered that cold night so long ago in that awful little flat in the Bronx. How she'd looked when she'd come through the door, lean and sleek and impossibly tempting. How she'd looked at *him*, as if she didn't know if he was a nightmare or a dream.

Maybe he'd been both. But she'd turned all of his nightmares on their heads, one after the next. She did it every day.

Liliana Agustin had long since come into her own. She had her mother's eye for a perfect line and her father's business sense, which made her indispensable to the company within a very short time. She was the peerless gem Izar had imagined she'd become; she was hailed as a visionary across the whole of the planet, and she only seemed to glow brighter by the day. And yet she was still happy to roll around on the floor in laughing heaps with their children, as if there was nothing the least bit pedigreed about her.

More than all this, she was his. Always and forever his.

And she'd been keeping something from him.

"I know you're there," she said without looking up from her work. "You storm beautifully, my love, but never quietly."

*"Gatita."* Her name was a command, and all these years later she still obeyed it, looking up at him. He smiled as he moved into the room. "I think you have something to tell me, do you not?"

"That depends. What do you *think* I have to tell you?"

Izar stopped beside her chair and pulled her to her feet, catching her against him, where she still fit. Where she would always fit.

"If I ask again," he murmured as he dropped his mouth to hers, "there will be consequences."

"Well," she said, tilting her head back to look at him, "you could say we're already chock-full of consequences." Her gaze danced with that mischief he adored. *"Sir."*

Once upon a time he'd called that defiance. Now he knew it was love.

He only lifted a brow in response, and Liliana laughed.

"Twins, Izar," she told him, her voice soft

with wonder. "We're having twins." She slid her hands up to his chest and rested them there. "And I know you didn't want that. I remember you thundering on horribly about empires and inheritances and only two—"

"I want you," Izar said, with utter certainty straight through to his bones. "I want them. I want everything."

Her smile was so bright he thought it might blind him, and he didn't care. She wound her arms around his neck and she pressed herself to him, and she was his. All this time, all they'd done, and Liliana was still entirely his.

And he loved her so much it hurt.

"Don't you see?" she asked, her beautiful eyes shining. "This is everything. Right here. This is our happy ending, Izar. We get to live it every day."

And finally, forever, Izar believed.

* * * * *

*If you enjoyed this story, check out these
other great reads from Caitlin Crews:*
**THE RETURN OF THE DI SIONE WIFE
EXPECTING A ROYAL SCANDAL
CASTELLI'S VIRGIN WIDOW**
*Available now!*

*And don't miss these other*
**ONE NIGHT WITH CONSEQUENCES**
*themed stories:*
**CLAIMING HIS CHRISTMAS
CONSEQUENCE**
*by Michelle Smart*
**THE SHEIKH'S BABY SCANDAL**
*by Carol Marinelli*
*Available now!*

# LARGER-PRINT BOOKS!
## GET 2 FREE LARGER-PRINT NOVELS PLUS
## 2 FREE GIFTS!

**☰HARLEQUIN®**

*Romance*

### From the Heart, For the Heart

---

**YES!** Please send me 2 FREE LARGER-PRINT Harlequin® Romance novels and my 2 FREE gifts (gifts are worth about $10). After receiving them, if I don't wish to receive any more books, I can return the shipping statement marked "cancel." If I don't cancel, I will receive 4 brand-new novels every month and be billed just $5.09 per book in the U.S. or $5.49 per book in Canada. That's a savings of at least 15% off the cover price! It's quite a bargain! Shipping and handling is just 50¢ per book in the U.S. and 75¢ per book in Canada.* I understand that accepting the 2 free books and gifts places me under no obligation to buy anything. I can always return a shipment and cancel at any time. Even if I never buy another book, the two free books and gifts are mine to keep forever.

119/319 HDN GHWC

| Name | (PLEASE PRINT) | |
|---|---|---|
| Address | | Apt. # |
| City | State/Prov. | Zip/Postal Code |

Signature (if under 18, a parent or guardian must sign)

### Mail to the **Reader Service**:
**IN U.S.A.:** P.O. Box 1867, Buffalo, NY 14240-1867
**IN CANADA:** P.O. Box 609, Fort Erie, Ontario L2A 5X3
**Want to try two free books from another line?**
Call 1-800-873-8635 or visit www.ReaderService.com.

* Terms and prices subject to change without notice. Prices do not include applicable taxes. Sales tax applicable in N.Y. Canadian residents will be charged applicable taxes. Offer not valid in Quebec. This offer is limited to one order per household. Not valid for current subscribers to Harlequin Romance Larger-Print books. All orders subject to credit approval. Credit or debit balances in a customer's account(s) may be offset by any other outstanding balance owed by or to the customer. Please allow 4 to 6 weeks for delivery. Offer available while quantities last.

**Your Privacy**—The Reader Service is committed to protecting your privacy. Our Privacy Policy is available online at www.ReaderService.com or upon request from the Reader Service.

We make a portion of our mailing list available to reputable third parties that offer products we believe may interest you. If you prefer that we not exchange your name with third parties, or if you wish to clarify or modify your communication preferences, please visit us at www.ReaderService.com/consumerchoice or write to us at Reader Service Preference Service, P.O. Box 9062, Buffalo, NY 14240-9062. Include your complete name and address.

HRLP15

# LARGER-PRINT BOOKS!
## GET 2 FREE LARGER-PRINT NOVELS PLUS
## 2 FREE GIFTS!

**HARLEQUIN®**

# INTRIGUE
## BREATHTAKING ROMANTIC SUSPENSE

# WESTERN (WP) PROMISES

**YES!** Please send me **The Western Promises Collection** in Larger Print. This collection begins with 3 FREE books and 2 FREE gifts (gifts valued at approx. $14.00 retail) in the first shipment, along with the other first 4 books from the collection! If I do not cancel, I will receive 8 monthly shipments until I have the entire 51-book Western Promises collection. I will receive 2 or 3 FREE books in each shipment and I will pay just $4.99 US/ $5.89 CDN for each of the other four books in each shipment, plus $2.99 for shipping and handling per shipment. *If I decide to keep the entire collection, I'll have paid for only 32 books, because 19 books are FREE! I understand that accepting the 3 free books and gifts places me under no obligation to buy anything. I can always return a shipment and cancel at any time. My free books and gifts are mine to keep no matter what I decide.

272 HCN 3070 472 HCN 3070

| | | |
|---|---|---|
| Name | (PLEASE PRINT) | |
| Address | | Apt. # |
| City | State/Prov. | Zip/Postal Code |

Signature (if under 18, a parent or guardian must sign)

## Mail to the **Reader Service**:
**IN U.S.A.:** P.O. Box 1867, Buffalo, NY 14240-1867
**IN CANADA:** P.O. Box 609, Fort Erie, Ontario L2A 5X3

* Terms and prices subject to change without notice. Prices do not include applicable taxes. Sales tax applicable in N.Y. Canadian residents will be charged applicable taxes. This offer is limited to one order per household. All orders subject to approval. Credit or debit balances in a customer's account(s) may be offset by any other outstanding balance owed by or to the customer. Please allow 4 to 6 weeks for delivery. Offer available while quantities last. Offer not available to Quebec residents.